"You pushed me."

"I was nine."

"I was humiliated."

He coughed to cover a full-blown laugh. "I'm sorry."

"You are not. And you were not sorry then either."

Choking back his laughter, he grabbed her upper arm. "Please, Livvy, I'm sorry. We were children and I couldn't resist the temptation of…of…"

With cheeks flaming, she fisted her fingers. "I could have drowned."

"Livvy, that was nearly ten years ago. We were children. Can't we start over?"

The only thing she wanted to start over was his foot. With a hard yank she slapped the reins on the horse's rump and nearly got her wish as the wagon lurched ahead. Whit jumped out of the way.

Expecting to see an impish grin plastered on his face, she frowned at the pain gripping his features. Maybe she *had* run over his foot. She pulled on the reins, but the barn-soured horse would not be deterred and continued forward.

It was just as well, for stinging regret watered her eyes and blurred her vision, and she would not let Whit Hutton see her cry.

Books by Davalynn Spencer

Love Inspired Heartsong Presents

The Rancher's Second Chance
The Cowboy Takes a Wife
Branding the Wrangler's Heart

DAVALYNN SPENCER's

love of writing has taken her from the city crime beat and national rodeo circuit to college classrooms and inspirational publication. When not writing romance or teaching, she enjoys speaking at women's retreats. She and her husband have three children and four grandchildren and make their home on Colorado's Front Range with a Queensland heeler named Blue. To learn more about Davalynn visit her website at www.davalynnspencer.com.

DAVALYNN SPENCER

Branding the Wrangler's Heart

HEARTSONG
PRESENTS

Recycling programs
for this product may
not exist in your area.

LOVE INSPIRED BOOKS

ISBN-13: 978-0-373-48709-7

BRANDING THE WRANGLER'S HEART

Have mercy upon me, O God, according to
thy lovingkindness: according unto the multitude
of thy tender mercies blot out my transgressions.
Wash me throughly from mine iniquity, and
cleanse me from my sin.
—*Psalms* 51:1–2

For all who entrust their hearts to God's unfailing love.

Chapter 1

Fremont County, Colorado, 1879

Whit Hutton stood in the stirrups and eyed the rimrock. His buckskin's ears swiveled toward a deep fissure, its nostrils flared for scent.

No padded foot dislodged the loose shale. No yellow eye glinted from the shadows, no tail whipped in the cool predawn. But she was there.

He settled back and heeled the buckskin up the ledge that hugged the cliff face. Oro took the incline at a cautious clip, more bighorn mountain sheep than horse. Whit let the gelding find its way while he kept his eyes on the rimrock and one hand at the ready.

His father's Colt lay holstered on his right hip, and a Winchester rested easy in the saddle scabbard. Trouble was, Whit didn't know what he'd need. If he spotted the lion from the canyon floor, he'd take it with the rifle. But if he rode up on its lair and forced a confrontation, he'd do better with the handgun.

And if the cat got the jump on him, it'd be too late for either one.

The back of his neck crawled. Feline eyes were watching.

Two calf carcasses in as many weeks proved an old lion stalked the herd—one too slow for a swift pronghorn or whitetail deer. It needed easy pickin's, and Hubert Baker's cow-calf operation appeared to be the chosen chuck wagon.

Oro heaved them up and over the edge and Whit reined around for a view of Wilson Creek bottom. The sleeping Bar-HB covered the stream-fed valley and several thousand acres of unseen park, timber ridges and rocky ravines. Baker, Whit, two other hands and three hundred cow-calf pairs called it home.

Lately, so did Baker's granddaughter, Olivia Hartman.

He turned his head toward a distant, rhythmic *ping,* not surprised that the echo carried so far on the clear air this early. Train barons were fighting for the narrow right-of-way up the Arkansas River canyon, and crews with both the Denver and Rio Grande and the Atchison, Topeka and Santa Fe were racing to lay track through the Royal Gorge. Only one railway would fit where sheer granite shot a thousand feet straight up from the river. And that rail owner would benefit mightily from the lucrative Leadville silver strikes.

While rich men pawed the earth and lawyers bandied, ranchers like Hubert Baker were still driving their cattle to mining camps a few at a time or in herds to Pueblo or the Denver railhead. Ten days of dust-eating trail, that one.

He shifted and the saddle leather squeaked. At least he didn't ride drag anymore—not since Baker crippled himself and put Whit in charge. Which meant Buck and Jody Perkins ate dirt on the drives the way Whit had when he was a young upstart. With no ma or pa of their own, the towheaded Perkins boys were happy enough to get chuck and a bed in the bunkhouse.

At least they hadn't lit out after easy money laying track for the feuding railroad companies.

The sun broke free, climbed Whit's back and jumped into the valley. He looked over his shoulder, dipped his brim against the new light, and turned Oro toward the ranch house and breakfast. The cat had eaten. Now it was their turn.

His stomach snarled and he hoped Livvy had whipped up some of her white gravy. She'd come to the ranch after her grandmother's death a month previous, and the little gal could fix up biscuits and gravy better than anything Whit had ever tasted. 'Cept his ma's cooking, of course. Couldn't beat the preacher's wife's potbelly biscuits, as Pa called them.

Guilt snagged a rib as Whit tied Oro at the house rail and walked around back to the washstand. He hadn't been home in three months, and he suspected his parents and little sister held it against him. But he had responsibilities now. He couldn't be traipsin' off to Cañon City whenever he wanted.

His spurs jangled against the kitchen floor and he continued through to the dining room where the Perkins brothers were already elbow deep in steak and eggs. Baker had insisted his hired hands eat at the house since his beloved Ruth passed. The old rancher was lonely. Whit could see it in his eyes when he looked at Livvy, a younger image of her mother, Hannah, Baker's only child. Whit used to tease the pigtailed girl at church picnics when her family visited from Denver. But he hadn't figured on scrawny Olivia Hartman growing up to be such a good cook. And a beauty to boot.

"You wash?" She leveled her blue eyes at him, ready to fire if he gave the wrong answer.

"Yes, ma'am. Right out back at the washstand. Even used soap this time."

Jody grunted but didn't stop chewing to comment.

"Hands." She leaned slightly forward, demanding he lift his callused fingers to her pretty little nose.

He pulled hard to draw a wounded look across his face. "You don't believe me?"

His mouth must have twitched, for she straightened to take the plate back to the kitchen. He jerked his hands out, palms up, and stepped as close as he could and still be the gentleman his parents raised.

Livvy sniffed, and her eyes smiled if her lips didn't. "Good." She set the plate on the table to the right of Baker, who sat at the head, and retreated to the kitchen.

Whit watched her disappear through the doorway. Someday he'd be sharing his meals in private with a woman like that.

"See any tracks?" Baker cut into a biscuit and sopped it in gravy.

Whit hung his hat on the chair back and took his seat. "No, sir. Too much shale in those bluffs to leave track. But I found her latest kill in the cottonwoods, half covered with leaves and brush."

He gulped his coffee, welcomed the kick. "But she was up there this morning. I could feel her."

Buck snorted. "You'll feel her all right. Just as soon as she leaps down on that buckskin o' yours and snaps your neck in two."

"Won't happen." Whit cut his steak and met Buck's jab with a poker face. "She's waitin' for a corn-fed one. Like you."

Jody choked on a piece of meat and grabbed his coffee, sloshing most of it onto his plate in the process.

Baker didn't join the fun as he usually did and his sober-
ness dampened the younger men's humor. Whit laid down
his fork and took up his coffee. The boss had something
on his mind and Whit'd just as soon hear it straight-out.

Livvy stood at the stove and wiped her hands on her
apron. Pop wasn't his jovial self this morning. She had
hoped the men could wheedle him into a better humor,
but their good-natured bantering wasn't breaking through
the dour mood he'd carried home from town yesterday.

She stirred the gravy in wide, slow circles, listening
for Pop's voice. It came low and tense, and she stilled the
spoon to concentrate on his words.

"I'm sure you all know about the feuding that's been
going on over the railway the last couple of years."

Knives and forks scraped against her grandmother's
Staffordshire china, and a coffee cup clinked on its saucer. No one spoke, and she imagined the others nodding
somberly.

"I don't want my men getting mixed up in any rail
war." Pop's voice carried an edge. "This blasted railroad
business is going to get someone killed and it better not
be any of you."

Someone cleared his throat. Whit, she guessed, who
usually spoke for all the hired hands.

"We're too busy," Whit said. "Gathering starts today
and I figure we'll be branding for three or four days. We
don't have the time or notion to be riding up that canyon
taking potshots at our neighbors."

Pop cursed and Livvy clapped a hand over her mouth.

"That's the problem," he said. "Those train barons have
called in outside guns and they're offering money to any
man that will sign on with them."

"Which side?"

The heavy silence meant Pop was staring a hole through

young Jody, the only one foolish enough to ask such a question.

A throat cleared. "Not that I'm thinkin' on joining them, mind you. I was just curious, that's all."

"Both sides."

A cup slammed into its saucer and Livvy flinched. She had only eight of the original twelve left, and the way Pop and these cowhands treated her grandmother's lovely blue-and-white china, she'd have no unchipped cups by summer's end. Tin suited them better, but at the dining table Pop insisted on the "good dishes." A tribute to his beloved Ruthie.

Chair legs combed the carpet as someone stood.

"You can count on us," Whit said. "We work for this outfit, not some railroad company."

Buck and Jody quickly agreed and flatware clattered against plates.

Livvy hurried to the sink, filled a dishpan and set it on the stove, grateful again that her grandfather had the convenience of an indoor hand pump.

Pop and the boys made their way through the kitchen, thanking her as always. Whit went out the front. She checked the other water pan already on the stove and returned to the dining room to clear the table. Through the lace curtain she saw Whit at the hitching rail, adjusting Oro's cinch. She moved to the window to watch him—something she did too often of late. Comfortable in the knowledge that he couldn't see her through the lacework, she wrapped her arms around her waist and studied his profile.

Dark and angular, his jaw shadowed with stubble. He was still lean but no longer the gangly boy who'd chased her in the churchyard. So different, yet so much the same as he had been during those growing-up years.

How did he see her now? As the skinny little girl who'd

begged him to push her in the swing and cried when he teased her? Or as a woman who had lost that child's heart to hero worship years ago?

He looked at the window. Livvy sucked in her breath and tightened her arms. She held her place, afraid to move and give herself away. A slow, easy smile tipped his mouth and he nodded once. Then he gathered the reins, swung into the saddle, and touched his hat brim before riding away.

Her vision darkened and she swayed. Reaching for a ladder-back chair, she gasped for air, her temples throbbing. This had to stop. She couldn't spend all summer holding her breath every time Whit Hutton looked at her.

She finished clearing the table, set a small leftover steak on the sideboard, and covered it with a napkin. Then she carefully placed the china in the dishpan and checked through the kitchen window for the men's whereabouts. Satisfied they were busy elsewhere, she grabbed a sharp knife and went out the front door.

An overgrown lilac bush billowed with deep purple blooms beside the dining room window. Carefully she cut three bunches and held them to her nose as she walked to the hitching rail. Glancing at the barn and bunkhouse, she turned to face the window. The lace curtains blocked her view of the chair where she had stood. Convinced that Whit could not have seen her through the sheer fabric, she went inside to search for a vase among her grandmother's collection.

The heavy oak door opened right into the dining room with no formal entry hall. The ranch house had grown out each end of the original square-log cabin, spreading into a comfortable home. A small porch announced the entrance, but Mama Ruth had never bemoaned the informality. She had directed her British ancestral conventions to more important things.

Like decor.

The Bar-HB might be a working cattle ranch, but Ruth Baker had swept a generous hand through her house where furniture and carpets, crystal and china were concerned. Livvy chose a lovely hand-painted vase from an ornate curio cabinet. She fussed with the heady blooms, slicing off the bottom of one bunch so its heart-shaped leaves cupped over the vase's lip. Several four-point blossoms dropped to the tablecloth and the rich perfume filled the room.

Mama Ruth had loved lilacs, and every window in the rambling house had a bush nearby that bloomed profusely from late spring into early summer—gentle lavender, brilliant white or deep purple. Even the dainty detail that edged the vase replicated the delicate blooms.

Livvy removed the soiled cloth to reveal the fine cherrywood table and stepped back to view the lilacs.

Whit could not possibly have seen her. So why did he act as if he knew she was there? How full of himself he was, assuming she stood at the window. That arrogant air had not changed one bit since their childhood.

She glanced down at the simple bodice of her blue calico and the full white apron that covered her skirt. Had it shown through the curtain?

Or had he *felt* her eyes on him?

Chapter 2

Whit reined Oro in behind the barn, jumped down and hurried through the side door to watch from the barn's shadowed innards. Sure enough, Livvy came outside and set to cutting purple flowers off the bush by the dining room window.

He laughed under his breath as she held the blooms to her nose and walked to the hitching rail, only to turn and face the house.

She didn't think he could see her through those frilly curtains. And he wouldn't have if she hadn't been wearing that white apron. It stood out like a bright square patch against the dark room. He hadn't been able to see her face, or even a faint outline of her form. But he'd seen the apron, and who else wore one at the ranch?

His chest swelled against his work shirt and he chuckled as he returned to Oro.

Miss Olivia Hartman had her sights on him.

Which brought to mind the lion on the rimrock and all

the work that needed tending to. He didn't have time to be thinking about grown-up Livvy with her yellow hair and sky-filled eyes. Three hundred mamas and their calves were grazing this spread, and he and Buck and Jody had to gather them for branding. And they needed to get it done quick enough to keep Baker from joining them and bustin' himself up even more.

The man never had said exactly what happened, but the way he favored his right leg, Whit guessed he'd tried to peel one too many broncs.

That's what the younger fellas were for.

Whit turned Oro for the nearest arroyo, where he'd told Buck and Jody to start. They'd hunt for pairs and drive those they found into the lower corral. Working their way into the rough country, they'd gather in bunches and cut and brand as they went.

He set his heels to Oro and they clipped along a streambed and turned off toward a red-rock patch jutting from the valley floor. Just ahead, Buck and Jody flanked a juniper cluster, hollering and slapping coiled ropes against their chaps. Whit circled behind them and took down his rope. He gave a whoop and jumped the old cow out of the thicket. Two calves followed close on her tail.

Buck whirled his mount away as the cow swung her wide horns. Jody took in after her at a trot and Whit joined the brothers as they pushed the threesome to the corrals.

"That was close," Whit said.

Buck grinned. "She's a snorty one for sure. Glad I was watchin' her close. Don't need a gutted horse or a hole in my leg."

Exactly why Whit didn't want Baker gathering stock. A good cowman through and through was Hubert Baker, except when it came to admitting his age and his bum leg. Grief over his wife's death was also carving a notch in him, and now he had a burr under his saddle over the train war. Rarely had Whit heard him swear, and doing so at the table—with Livvy in earshot—was even more of a puzzle. The stubby little man's mind wouldn't be on the work out here, and Buck wasn't the only cowboy who didn't need to take a hookin' this summer.

The homebound parade drew a bellow at the red-rock patch, and Jody loped off to pick up two more head and their calves. By the time Whit and the Perkins boys closed in on the outlying pens, they'd flushed twelve cows from the near canyon. Only one was barren. Pretty good return.

By noon, twenty head were branded and turned out from the holding pens at the windmill. Whit dismounted, left his hat on his saddle horn and stuck his head under the trough pump. Cold mountain water gushed out over his neck and down his back. He scrubbed his face and hands and flung his hair back. Wiping his face on his shirtsleeve, he turned in time to see Livvy driving up in the buckboard, a sun bonnet hiding her best features.

Buck and Jody took their turns at the pump and got into a shoving match. Suited Whit just fine. Gave him more time alone with Livvy.

Drying his hands on his pants, he hurried to the wagon to help her. She wrapped the reins around the brake handle and gathered her skirt in one hand, then took Whit's with the other as she climbed down the front wheel. He thought about looping her narrow waist with his hands and lifting her down, but if he knew Livvy Hartman, she'd wallop him good with both fists while he was at it. The idea quirked his mouth and he frowned to cover his thoughts.

"What now, Whitaker Caleb Hutton?" Two daring eyes challenged him from inside the shadowed bonnet.

Full given names, was it? "Watch your step there, Olivia Hannah Hartman."

She glared at him and he glared back. How often had she beaten him at a staring match when they were children?

"Did you bring dinner?" Jody sauntered over. "I'm so hungry I could eat my saddle blanket."

"Then go to it, brother. Leaves more for the rest of us." Buck jerked Jody's hat over his eyes as he walked by.

The bantering snatched Livvy's attention. If Whit didn't need the Perkinses' help with the branding, he would thrash both boys into a stupor.

A midday meal during roundup was a treat. Usually they worked clear through and didn't eat again until evening. Livvy walked to the end of the wagon, where she dropped the back railing into a makeshift sideboard and pulled out two baskets and a covered crock. From one basket she withdrew forks and tin plates and cups. The other basket held fried chicken that licked Whit's nose as soon as Livvy folded back the checkered cloth.

Livvy heaped three plates with crisp chicken, potato salad and molasses cookies, and then dipped lemonade from the crock into three tin mugs. Whit waited for her to help herself to the meal but she didn't.

"You eating?"

She dusted her hands on the ever-present apron. "Don't worry about me. Just have at it. I'll be fine."

Livvy Hartman was fine all right, but she'd picked up a burr like her granddad. She turned and walked off toward a pine and aspen cluster, leaving Whit and the brothers to enjoy her handiwork alone.

"What'd you do now?" Jody shoved the meat end of a drumstick in his mouth and pulled out the bone.

Whit resisted the urge to punch him. If the kid choked on a hunk of chicken, they'd be short-handed.

A blue patch at the clearing's edge caught Livvy's eye and she hiked her skirt to walk through the ankle-deep grass. Whit Hutton made her want to say what Pop had said at breakfast, and her mother would have a fit for sure if she knew it. He was more irritating as a man than he'd ever been as a boy. Could she last six months isolated in these mountains with no one to talk to but her grieving grandfather and his sassy-mouthed foreman who was too big for his britches?

She stooped to cup a blossom in her hand and peeked back at the wagon. Whit leaned against the buckboard drinking lemonade. His britches fit him just fine. Blood rushed to her cheeks, from bending over no doubt, so she knelt before the patch and focused on the delicate petals.

The flowers weren't blue at all but more lavender, like Mama Ruth's lilacs. She'd not seen anything like them in Denver, but living in the city offered little opportunity to ride into the high country. Up until now, schoolwork, helping her mother at the parsonage and playing the organ for Daddy's congregation had filled most of her days. She had jumped at the offer to escape to Pop's ranch—without any thought of what awaited her.

"How beautiful," she whispered as she leaned over to breathe in their fragrance.

"They're columbines."

Catching herself before she tumbled onto her face, she looked back to see Whit towering over her. A grin lifted his mouth and his hat perched on his head like the comb of a cocky rooster. Peeved that he had walked up on her while her backside was in the air, she dropped to the ground and assumed a more dignified arrangement.

Whit laughed.

"And tell me, please, what you find so humorous."

He took his hat off and sank smoothly to a cross-legged position. "No need to worry, Miss Hartman. Only a memory that tickled my funny bone." His dark eyes snapped.

Livvy curled her fingers in the grass. She made to stand and he reached for her arm. The smirk vanished and remorse took its place.

"Don't go."

Surprised by his candor, she sank down. He released her arm.

She pushed her bonnet back and let it hang on the wide strings tied beneath her chin.

"I just thought you might like to know what these flowers are called. I've seen 'em all white like snow, higher up in the mountains."

Livvy relaxed and looked again at the wildflowers. Each one bore a white face, yellow center and long claw-like growths that tapered from the bottom of every lavender petal.

Whit picked one and twirled it slowly in front of her. "See these long tubes? They're called spurs and they hold the nectar that draws hummingbirds and bees."

How did a cowboy know about flowers? She shot a quick glance his way and caught him squinting at the ridge above them.

"Spurs, you say?"

Her remark brought his gaze back to her and his features softened. "Yes, ma'am. Kinda like us cowboys." For a moment he looked exactly as she remembered him from her previous visits, before he worked for her grandfather. But now he was somehow more…handsome?

"Well, that's very nice." She fussed with her skirt, making sure it covered her ankles.

He offered her the flower.

She took it and raised it to her nose. Perhaps the taste attracted the hummingbirds rather than the scent. "So you could call it a cowboy flower, I suppose."

"*You* could call it anything you want."

His emphasis shot heat back into her face and this time she succeeded in standing before he stopped her. With one hand she shook out her skirt and smoothed her apron.

"If you and the others are finished, I'll be heading back to the house."

He stood with an inscrutable expression, his jaw set like stone, his eyes flat. "Suit yourself."

Livvy cradled the fragile flower in her palm. The velvety spurs pricked her conscience and she rebuffed the guilty stab. She was simply being proper. She and Whit were no longer children who played hide-and-seek and—

She whirled on him and fought the impulse to shove him off his feet. "You…you…*scoundrel*."

Stunned and rooted in his tracks, he stared at her, clearly befuddled. "Pardon?"

"You scoundrel! I know what you were laughing at. I remember now—the day we were playing at the church house in Cañon City and I bent over the horse trough."

The slow smile pulled at his mouth and his eyes came to life. "I do believe I have never seen anyone madder."

She burned from the inside out. How dare he make light of her humiliation. Why had she ever forgiven him? "You pushed me."

"I was nine."

"I was humiliated."

He coughed to cover a full-blown laugh. "I'm sorry."

"You are not. And you were not sorry then, either."

Choking back his laughter, he grabbed her upper arm. "Please, Livvy, I'm sorry. We were children and I couldn't resist the temptation of…of…"

With cheeks flaming, she fisted her fingers. "I could have drowned."

"But I saved you." Humor and regret battled across his features and the former was winning.

Jerking away, she marched to the wagon.

Buck and Jody saw her coming and ran to their horses.

She threw the dishes in a basket, slammed the drop board against the wagon railing and locked it in place.

"Livvy—wait."

She would rather die. Lifting her skirt with one hand, she gripped the bench seat with the other and climbed up the wheel spokes.

Whit ran to the horse and grabbed its bridle. "Livvy, that was nearly ten years ago. We were children. Can't we start over?"

The only thing she wanted to start over was his foot. With a hard yank, she slapped the reins on the horse's rump and nearly got her wish as the wagon lurched ahead. Whit jumped out of the way.

Expecting to see an impish grin plastered on his face, she frowned at the pain gripping his features. Maybe she *had* run over his foot. She pulled on the reins, but the barn-soured horse would not be deterred and continued forward.

It was just as well, for stinging regret watered her eyes and blurred her vision, and she would not let Whit Hutton see her cry.

After a jostling quarter-mile ride, Livvy pulled around to the kitchen entrance and carried the baskets inside, making a second trip for the heavy crock. As she unloaded the dishes and set them in the sink, the crushed columbine fell to the floor.

She must have dropped it on a plate when she packed up.

She stooped to retrieve the bruised and broken flower, so delicate and once so lovely. Holding it against her bodice, she closed her eyes and let childish frustration and grown-up disappointment slip down her cheeks.

Chapter 3

Whit Hutton did not swear. "Not by heaven or earth," his preacher pa had taught him. But he sure enough knew a few colorful phrases he could let fly to fit the situation.

He gathered Oro's reins and swung into the saddle, looking to see which way the Perkins boys had fled. He hadn't even told them which draw to work next. Livvy had driven every logical thought and plan right out of his head.

Exasperating woman.

Scanning the ground, he spotted the print of the bar shoe on the back right of Buck's mount and followed the tracks. The brothers were loping their horses toward the next canyon, running scared from the storming fury of Miss Olivia Hartman.

He kicked Oro into a lope. Livvy was as bad as his sister, Marti, who still saw him as bothersome. What did he have to do to show Livvy he'd grown up and was as much a man as the next fella?

Stop teasing her.

He snorted. That'd be harder than jumping a maverick steer and not near as much fun. He should forget about Livvy, leave her uppity little self alone.

Priscilla Stockton came to mind. Now there was a more appreciating gal. She sure enough paid him heed the last Sunday he was at church—three months back. He was due for another trip to town, but not until after branding.

He eased Oro into a walk as they skirted a cholla cactus patch, and the hair on the back of his neck raised like a porcupine's quills. He peered up at the rimrock, tried to see into the shallow caves tucked under the top layer. His right hand slid to the Colt and Oro tensed beneath his legs, feeling Whit's apprehension. One ear swiveled to the right and one pointed straight ahead.

A lion attack in broad daylight was rare. Whit yanked that truth to the front of his mind and focused on the cattle they were hunting.

A strangled bawl caught his ear and he gave the gelding its head.

Jody had himself a stubborn one. He held his rope dallied around the saddle horn and the taut line stretched over the butt of his horse as he tried to drag the cow. Buck was slapping his chaps behind her but she choked down. Her eyes rolled white and her tongue hung out as she bellowed at her calf.

"Let up," Whit called as he neared the standoff. "Give her some air before that rope snaps and takes off the side of your face."

Apparently stunned by the idea, Jody eased his horse back and the cow lowered her head and sucked air. The calf made for dinner, taking a kick for it from its frustrated mother.

They pushed the pair out of the canyon, and on the way to the corrals Whit found a couple more. At this rate, it'd take a month to get the cattle in.

"You need a different horse, Jody. The mare's too small. It's a wonder that cow didn't drag you all the way to the top of Eight Mile Mountain." Jody looked as if his feelings were hurt. Better his feelings than his neck. "You and Buck ride to the upper park and cut out one of the bigger geldings."

After bunching and branding a few more out in the open, the brothers took off into the hills.

By the time the sun tucked in, Whit had driven a dozen pairs to the holding pens. In the morning, they'd brand and cut what they had, then head for the higher bunch grounds and start gathering there.

Whit unsaddled Oro, rubbed him down and turned him out in the pasture behind the house. The buckskin had earned his keep today. So had Whit, but Livvy Hartman's angry scowl sat sour on his gut. He had half a mind to turn in early and skip supper.

He slapped his hat against his leg. Baker would hunt him down if he didn't show, that was for certain, and the man didn't need any more worries on his mind.

How could one little blue-eyed gal stir up such a storm in Whit's belly? Even when they were children she'd needled him, driven him into fits with her pestering. Then if he got her good, she'd turn those tear-filled blues on him and he'd feel like a mangy cur. As he had today when she remembered him dunking her in the horse trough.

He chuckled in spite of himself. Served her right, trying to see her reflection in the still water. He just hadn't expected the prank to dog him the rest of his days. One little shove, and she hated him for life.

He had apologized, thanks to his mother nearly twisting his ear off. And Livvy had accepted, right there in the churchyard, her soaked dress clinging to her skinny legs, two yellow braids dripping water.

Without realizing it, he'd walked to the washstand on

the wide back porch. The kitchen window framed Livvy working at the table, peeling the root-cellar spuds he'd brought in yesterday morning.

The lamp on the table cast a yellow light against her hair, setting it to gold. His insides twisted at the thought of touching it—not yanking it the way he had as a boy, but filling his hands with it, burying his face in its softness.

Confounded woman had him all in a knot. One minute he regretted knowing her, and the next he wanted to take her in his arms.

He hung his hat on a nail, rolled up his sleeves and splashed cold water over his head, trying to wash away the image of Olivia Hartman. Lord, what was he going to do? The woman made him loco.

Livvy skinned the small potatoes and sliced them into a bowl. When she had it filled, she took it to the stove and dumped the slices into hot bacon grease in the big iron skillet. They spit and spattered and she set a lid half on and returned to the table. The peelings went into a tin she kept for chicken scraps and she set it on the back windowsill.

Outside a man bent over the washstand, splashing water on his face. With a gasp she jerked back. *Whit.*

She hurried to the stove, where she wouldn't have to face him when he came inside. She prayed he'd go straight to the dining room without stopping to make small talk or apologize. As if Whit Hutton would apologize.

The door opened and shut softly. Spurred boots crossed the bare kitchen floor and stopped a few feet away. She held her breath, bunched her apron in hand and lifted the lid on the potatoes, feigning distraction over supper. The boots continued into the dining room, where their steps muffled against her grandmother's imported carpet.

Livvy blew out a sigh and returned to the table, where she fell into a chair. Oh, Lord, she couldn't live all summer like this, tensing up every time Whit came around. Maybe she should leave, go back to Denver, and carry on with her normal, boring life. And abandon Pop?

Never. She slapped her hands on her apron. Those no-account cowboys didn't cook or tend a garden or gather eggs or feed the chickens. They barely kept the firewood stacked and the cow milked.

She pushed her hair off her forehead and stood with new resolve. The men had cleaned up every scrap of dinner today, so she sliced the leftover breakfast steak into the fried potatoes. Good thing she hadn't taken her canned-peach pie out to the bunch grounds, or they'd have nothing to go with their coffee tonight.

By the time Livvy had the table set and herself seated, Buck and Jody's absence hung like a cold lantern. She held out her right hand to Pop, buried her left one in her lap, and jerked her head down without looking across at Whit. Beneath her lashes she saw him withdraw his hand from the table where he had reached across for hers.

Pop cleared his throat. "Lord, we thank You for all You've blessed us with, this food and this ranch, and the work You've given us to do. Watch over us tonight, Lord. And bring the boys back safely. Amen."

"Amen." Livvy's quiet agreement matched Whit's exactly and she felt his eyes on her. Reaching for Pop's plate, she filled it with steak and potatoes and set it before him. Fixing her attention on the knot in Whit's gray neckerchief, she held her hand out, waiting for him to give her his plate. She waited until embarrassment forced her eyes to his face. He was staring at her without smirk or smile. Without anything. He handed her his plate and her heart plopped to her stomach as the potatoes hit the floral scene on Mama Ruth's blue-and-white china.

If she didn't eat, Pop would question her and she'd have to answer and what would she say? She spooned out a small helping of potatoes for herself. "Where *are* the boys, Pop?"

Baker looked to Whit, who picked up his fork and pinned an elbow on the table. "I sent them to the high park to cut out a gelding for Jody. He got himself lined out with a cow today that was bigger than that little mare he rides. I'm afraid he's going to get himself hurt."

Pop grunted and nodded his head as he herded sliced potatoes and steak around on his plate. "When was that?"

Whit set down his fork and reached for his coffee. "Late afternoon." He took a sip. "I probably should have had him wait until tomorrow, given them all day to get up to the herd."

"Do you think they'll cut out for the railroad?"

Livvy's fork stuck on her plate and she looked straight at Whit, who was staring at his food. "Before today I would have said no for certain. Now I'm prayin' they don't."

Since when did Whit Hutton pray? Even if his father *was* a preacher.

"There's a few wild head in with that herd, you know."

"I know." Whit frowned and stabbed his steak. "I should have gone with them."

"You can *should have* yourself into the grave, son. Don't do it. I do enough for both of us."

Livvy's heart squeezed at her grandfather's confession and she blinked rapidly to keep from tearing up at the table. He insisted almost daily that if he'd ridden for the doctor sooner, Mama Ruth might still be alive.

Might. Only God knew the answer to that.

A clatter at the kitchen door jerked Livvy to her feet. The Perkins brothers charged in stomping and slapping and laughing, two young giants dusting themselves off in the kitchen rather than outside at the washstand.

"You march right back out and wash up." Livvy straight-armed them both with a sharp turn of their shoulders and shoved them toward the door. Thank God, they weren't dead, or dragging along at the end of their ropes over rocks and down washes in the wake of those running horses.

"And don't you dare be stomping your dirty boots in this kitchen."

She returned to the dining room, filled two plates and poured coffee before taking her seat. Whit's stare burned her cheeks. She took a deep breath and met it with her own.

"Couldn't you even ask them if they were all right?"

Anger curled her fingers in her lap and she jutted her chin. "They are all right or they wouldn't be making such a ruckus. And they might as well learn now to clean up outside before they come in. We are not barbarians."

"Do you even know what that word means?"

Pop coughed and held a napkin to his mouth.

Certain that she'd fall off her chair if she didn't breathe, Livvy inhaled through her nose and held Whit's glare. How dare he?

The back door opened again, and two quieter young men came through the kitchen and into the dining room. They nodded first at Livvy, then at Baker and Whit before taking their seats.

"This smells mighty good, Miss Olivia." Jody plunged into his food and Buck kicked him under the table and jerked his head at the napkin beside Jody's plate. The younger brother snatched it to his lap and cut a side glance at Livvy before returning to his meal.

Their antics drew everyone's attention and Livvy couldn't decide who had given in and looked away first: Whit or her.

"Did you find a mount?" Whit held his cup in both hands, both elbows on the table.

Livvy held her tongue.

"Sure did," Buck said with his mouth full.

Livvy shook her head. The Perkins boys had no manners at all.

"A real nice black with a white blaze."

"That'd be Shade." Pop forked a piece of steak. "Good horse if you take the hump out of him every morning."

Jody looked up with his mouth open and his fork poised in midair. "Huh?"

Whit quirked a half grin. "I'll start him for you tomorrow and in a couple of days he'll get used to you. Either that or you'll get used to the ground."

Pop grunted a near laugh and Livvy almost wanted to thank Whit for lightening the moment.

"What took you so long?" Whit set his empty cup in the saucer and glanced at Livvy, the dregs of good humor in his eyes.

She filled his cup and Pop's, and went to the kitchen for the pie.

"Them horses can run," Buck said between bites. "Took us all afternoon to cut the black out. Rode back in near dark and by the time we got him in the corral and watered it was well past."

More grunts from Pop, and Livvy whispered a prayer of thanks. Those crazy Perkins brothers were worth her trouble if they could help keep her grandfather from grieving his life away. Pie server in hand, she paused before the doorway and peeked at Whit from the safety of the kitchen. Maybe she should cut him some slack, as she'd heard her grandfather say. Give him the chance he'd asked for today.

She picked up the pie and entered the dining room just as the back door flew open.

Chapter 4

"Please, can you help us?"

Whit leaped from his chair at the panicked request and almost trampled Livvy in his hurry.

Delores Overton stood against the night, struggling to hold up her near-grown son. Pale and unconscious, the youth sagged against her. On his left shoulder, a hoof-sized bloodstain oozed around a small hole in his shirt. Too small for a cow horn.

Whit took the boy.

"He's been shot." She began to sob and covered her face with her hands. Livvy hurried over and wrapped her arms around the woman.

"Bring me some chairs," Whit hollered.

Pop shoved his chair through the dining room door and angled it beneath the limp body as Whit sat the boy in it.

Buck and Jody stood gaping, slack-jawed.

"Chairs," Whit demanded.

Jumping at the clipped order, they delivered their chairs

and stepped back as Baker and Whit stretched Tad Overton across the three seats. Livvy gave Delores a reassuring hug then gathered clean rags and towels. She poured warm kettle water into a crockery bowl and dipped a rag in it.

Delores swayed on her feet and Whit caught her. "Mr. Baker, please take Mrs. Overton to the dining room and have her sit down on the settee."

After she left the room, Whit opened Tad's shirt and peeled it off his left shoulder. Livvy applied the warm rag to his wound without hesitation. Her face showed only compassion and clear thinking. No panic, no revulsion.

Whit was not surprised.

"Someone needs to ride for the doctor," Livvy said.

Buck stepped forward. "I will."

"No." Pop came back to the kitchen and everyone looked at him with the same question.

"We need to take him to the doctor. It will be faster." Pop turned to the Perkins boys. "Buck, you harness Bess to the buckboard and fill the back with straw. Jody, take care of Mrs. Overton's horse or wagon or whatever she's got out there. Whit, take the quilt off my bed. You'll find blankets in the chest by my door. We'll make him as comfortable as possible for the trip."

Whit hadn't seen his boss come this alive since before Ruth died.

Livvy continued with the compresses. Whit laid a hand on her shoulder. "Thank you."

The look she gave him made him weak in the knees.

"I'll go with you," she said. "All that jostling is liable to make him bleed more."

Baker stoked the cookstove, brought the coffeepot from the dining room and set it on the fire. "Hurry," he said to Whit. "Delores and I will stay here."

As Whit passed by, Pop grabbed his arm. "Take it as fast as you can. It'll be a long ten miles." He lowered his voice. "But I don't think he can make it horseback across the open country."

"We'll make it," Whit said, offering a promise he didn't know if he could keep.

Tad moaned and Livvy smoothed back his tousled hair. Something in her manner stirred Whit. He turned away and hurried through the rambling house to the bedroom at the far end.

He recognized the log-cabin pattern in the quilt on Baker's oak bed, thanks to his ma's handiwork, and wasted no time stripping it off. Then he lifted the trunk lid and found extra blankets and other linen a woman kept on hand. He took three blankets, set the lid down and headed outside.

Buck and Jody were pitching straw in the back of the buckboard and Whit stretched two blankets across the top. "Wait out here and help me get him in the wagon."

Delores had returned to the kitchen and sat on a stool pulled close to her son's head. She stroked his brow and murmured low as Livvy finished knotting a strip around the boy's shoulder.

"Looks like you've done this before." Whit watched her, waited for her reply.

She picked up the remaining towels, stuffed them in a satchel and gathered her cloak from a peg by the door. "You could say that."

He wanted to know more, but now was not the time.

Stooping to slip his arms beneath Tad, he lifted him and flinched as the boy's head lobbed back. At least he felt no pain.

Whit stopped at the door and faced Delores. "How long ago did he come home?"

"Just after dark." A sudden sob caught her breath and she held a hand to her mouth. "At first he wouldn't tell me what happened, but I guessed it." She looked into Whit's eyes, searching for hope. "He was up at Texas

Creek, on the railbed. The Santa Fe is paying three dollars a day to lay track. He said it was quicker money than waiting to sell our steers this fall."

Her voice broke on the last word and she covered her face.

Pop swore under his breath, opened the door for Whit and stopped Livvy on her way out. "Keep your seat, because he'll be runnin' that horse. But you'll be safe with Whit—I'd trust him with my life."

Baker's words tightened Whit's throat as he lifted Tad to the Perkins boys, who each grabbed an end. He hopped into the wagon bed and tucked a blanket and the quilt tight around the boy. Then he held out his hand to Livvy as she climbed up the back wheel.

"Will you be warm enough with that light wrap?"

Her mouth curved in a gentle smile and she laid a hand on his arm. "I'll be fine, Whit. You just give Bess what for and get us to Doc's."

He covered her hand with his and squeezed, then shoved his hat down tighter and stepped over the bench.

The Perkins boys stood like orphaned calves watching the herd leave them behind.

"No gathering till I get back," Whit told them. "You can ride to the Overtons' and check on things for the widow." He slapped the reins and then pulled up and pegged Buck with a solemn stare.

"You're in charge. If anything goes wrong while we're gone, I'll blame you."

Even in the faint light from the kitchen window, he could see Buck's face tighten.

"You can count on us." The boy stretched to his full height, all sixteen years of it.

Whit looked over his shoulder to be certain Livvy was seated, and she offered him another gentle smile. He flicked the reins and Bess clopped forward.

* * *

Livvy pulled back the quilt's top corner and blanket and checked Tad's bandage. Not as much blood had seeped through as she'd expected. She tucked another folded rag beneath the toweling strip and pressed it in place.

"Hold on," Whit yelled over his shoulder. At the barn, he turned onto the ranch road, slapped the reins, and hollered at Bess.

The wagon lurched ahead, nearly throwing Livvy on her back. She reached for the seat and pulled herself forward. Turning, she leaned against the low board behind the bench, still close to her patient with his head at her knees. Thank goodness the boy was unconscious.

And boy he was. Couldn't be more than fifteen. She ran the back of her fingers across his downy cheeks, where no razor had ever traveled.

Moonlight full as near day spilled across Tad's features as well as the countryside—the rimrock ledges and pastures and close hills, all colorless in the gray light but clear to the eye. A coyote yipped in the distance. Livvy shivered, and pulled her cloak tighter.

Whit had questioned her comfort—an uncharacteristically gallant thing for him to do since he'd spent most of their childhood time together making her miserable. And how quickly he'd responded tonight. Even her grandfather had sparked to life issuing orders and taking charge. Did personal regret push him to insist they take Tad into town rather than wait for the doctor?

The boy moaned and thrashed his legs.

She stroked his cheek, felt the fever. "Hush now," she whispered close to his ear. "You rest and we'll be at Doc Mason's before you know it." She should have searched her grandmother's stores for laudanum, or even whiskey, but Tad's unconscious state had pushed such ministrations from her mind. Doc Mason would soon take over, though even at this breakneck pace, soon wasn't soon enough.

The wagon hit a hole and she bounced hard, falling across Tad. Ready to give Whit a piece of her mind, her ire vanished at the sight of his shirt stretched tight across his tense back and shoulders. He worked to keep them on the road and in one piece, but had not thought to bring himself a coat.

Livvy retucked the loosened quilt and settled herself against the board. *"I'd trust him with my life,"* Pop had said, his weathered face reflecting a need to reassure her.

Pop and Mama Ruth never had a son—only a daughter, her mother, Hannah. Other cattlemen had tried to buy Pop out over the years, but he'd held on through good markets and lean. Who was there to leave his spread to? Her mother? Growing up in these remote hills, she knew what to do. But her place was with Daddy, and he didn't know the first thing about running a cattle ranch. Besides, he'd never leave his Denver pastorate, unless of course the Lord called him elsewhere.

A new doubt shivered through Livvy. What if God called Daddy to another church? The thought of leaving what had always been home clenched her stomach. She could never live anywhere else, except maybe...

She pushed the notion aside and touched Tad's face again. Hot. Drawing back the quilt, she felt the heat in his shoulder, as well, and left a single blanket to cover him. She prayed he'd live to care for his widowed mother.

Pop had told Livvy about Delores Overton, how the woman's husband had died from a fall shortly after homesteading beneath Eight Mile Mountain. She had refused to leave even though Pop had offered to buy out her 160-acre claim and her few cows. She was determined to make a go of her dead husband's dream.

What choices would the widow have if she lost her only child?

Livvy tilted her head back and considered her own options if she found herself in a similar predicament. What would she do in such a place as Cañon City? And to whom would she turn?

Another bounce and she grabbed for the side rail. How much longer could Tad Overton take such a beating?

Thoughts of an unpredictable future pulled her into a shallow sleep, but soon a faster gait on a smoother surface awoke her. She straightened and looked around. They'd made the turn at the hogbacks and were on the west end of the road into Cañon City. Doc Mason's place was ahead on the right.

Whit slowed Bess to a walk and soon stopped before a small two-story house with dark shutters and fenced yard. Livvy felt Tad's forehead and looked up to see Whit watching her.

"I'm going to wake the doctor, then I'll be back for the boy."

Livvy nodded, amazed at the gentleness in Whit's voice. "The boy" was not that much younger than she and Whit.

Loud and prolonged knocking garnered an eventual light in an upstairs window, and soon Whit was climbing into the wagon. Doc Mason lowered the back, his unshouldered galluses hanging from his trousers.

Whit knelt on Tad's opposite side. "Grab the blanket beneath him and help me turn him sideways and drag him to the back."

Livvy complied and they managed to lay Tad along the edge, where earlier in the day she had laid dinner. Whit jumped down. She hiked her skirts to climb down but stopped at the sight of Whit's uplifted hands. Maybe it was the seriousness in his dark eyes that prompted her to lean over and place her hands on his shoulders as he encircled her waist and deftly set her on the ground. He held her eyes for a moment longer, then turned to cradle Tad in his arms and carry him through the front gate and into Doc Mason's home.

Flustered by Whit's conduct, she brushed the straw off her skirt, raised and locked the back rail, and checked to see if Whit had set the brake. Of course he had, and Bess's reins lay loosely around the handle.

In the shadowy yard, she paused to let her hair down, recoil and pin it against her neck. Then she smoothed the sides and shook out her skirt. The front door stood ajar, and she pushed it farther open and stepped into what appeared to be a waiting area. Closing the door softly behind her, she took in the simple furnishings, obviously bachelor's decor. No fine cabinet held crystal and china, no imported floral carpet covered the plank floor but instead a large braided rug, encircled by mismatched chairs hugging every wall. An empty fireplace yawned at one end and a small table and unlit lamp posed against the other.

For as long as Livvy could remember, Doc Mason had lived at this end of town, caring faithfully for local residents and those from outlying ranches. He'd brought babes into this world and escorted the dying to the next. With a quick breath she clasped her hands. He'd been at her grandmother's side, as well, but not soon enough in her grandfather's opinion.

Through an open doorway, she watched shadows move against a papered wall, heard low voices discuss Tad's condition. She stepped to the threshold and her nose flared at the smell of fresh blood. Funny she hadn't noticed it at the ranch house.

Tad lay on a long narrow table. Doc bent over his shoulder and Whit held a glass lamp close. He must have sensed her presence for he looked at her and nodded. No sly grin hitched his mouth, no teasing words crossed his lips. A thick line ran around his dark hair where his hat had permanently creased it, and the yellow light cut deep grooves between his brows. Livvy clenched her hands against the sudden urge to smooth away the worry and trail her fingertips along his roughening beard.

The telltale narrowing of her vision warned that she was holding her breath again. She inhaled deeply through her nose and rubbed her temples. *Breathtaking* was a word she'd not used much before coming to help her grandfather this summer, but his foreman was bringing it more and more to her mind in a most personal way.

Pop's quilt and blanket crumpled against a chair in the corner. For something to do, she gathered them and took them out to the parlor, where she picked off the straw and tossed it into the cold fireplace. Then she folded the blanket and quilt into neat orderly squares.

Why couldn't she do the same with her emotions where Whit Hutton was concerned?

Chapter 5

"Thank you, Doc. We'll square up with you when we come back for him, if that's all right." Whit shoved his hat on and shook the doctor's hand. He figured Baker would cover for the widow. If not, Whit had enough stashed in the bottom of his bedroll. There was no way he'd let Delores Overton pay for what her fool-headed son had done.

"That will be fine, Whit, but what are you going to do tonight?" He dried his hands and arms on a towel and hung it over a rod on the washstand. "It's a couple hours till daylight. I have an extra room upstairs, but only one, and with Miss Hartman…"

"Thank you kindly. I do appreciate it. But I'm taking Livvy, er, Miss Hartman to my folks' place. They'll have room at the parsonage and I can always sleep in the barn."

Mason rolled down his sleeves and shot a doubtful look over the top of his wire-rim spectacles.

Whit laughed. "Rest easy, Doc. The hayloft is only a little softer than Baker's bunkhouse."

Mason shook his head and rechecked the new dressing around Tad Overton's shoulder. "This is the first gunshot wound I've seen from the railway war they're fightin' in the canyon. I sure hope this is the worst of it."

"Me, too, Doc." Whit moved to the door. Blamed kid should have known better than to get mixed up in somebody else's fight, but money could turn a fella's head. Whit gritted his teeth. If the Perkins boys got dragged into it, he'd wear out their sorry hides.

On his way out of the surgery, he stopped in the doorway. Livvy slumped in a chair across the room, her head tipped back and her mouth open. He could get her lathered up over that—but he wouldn't. He'd spent enough of his life riding her about every little thing. He hadn't known any other way to get her attention when they were kids.

Things were different now. He was grown and so was she. It was time to be thinking like a man, and the first thing a man needed was a—

Livvy startled and sat upright. She clamped her jaw and narrowed her eyes. Her reaction put a hitch in his mouth even though he knew it would get her back up.

"Don't you dare laugh at me, Whitaker Hutton."

He frowned and screwed his hat down. "I am not laughing at you." He made for the front door, put gravel in his voice. "Come on. We're going to my folks' place. They'll put you up in the spare room and we'll go back to the ranch tomorrow. Doc wants Overton to stay here a day or two so he can keep an eye on him."

He opened the door and waited. Livvy stood and smoothed out her skirt.

"Where's your wrap?"

"In the wagon."

"I'll get it."

She marched past him. "That will not be necessary, thank you. I can get it myself."

Livvy circled round the buckboard, lifted her cloak from the back and shook out the straw. Then she draped the light wool over her shoulders, clambered up the wheel and scooted to the far end of the seat before he could climb aboard.

Infuriating woman.

He plopped down next to her and reached for the reins. He should have left her behind and brought Jody. But that half-broke bronc would have made a poor nurse. And he'd never smell as sweet as Livvy did right now. He cut a glance to the side. There she sat with her neck stiff as a sulled-up filly. Why couldn't she be more even tempered, like a seasoned gelding?

He coughed, covering a laugh that escaped at the outrageous comparison. Miss Olivia Hartman would whack him good if she knew he'd compared her to a horse.

Bess's hooves clopped against the hard-packed street and echoed off the sleeping storefronts. Whitaker's Mercantile had a new sign painted since he'd last been in town. His grandfather was getting up in years like Baker. He and his wife, Martha, had been running the store all Whit's life, and had often hinted at Whit taking it over.

He loved his grandparents dearly, but the thought of working every day indoors made his chest hurt. He had to be outside, in a saddle, free to cast his eye over the mountains and timber and parks the good Lord made.

He shuddered, and from the corner of his eye, saw Livvy glance at him. What made her switch so suddenly? Sweet one minute and sour the next. Was it him? Was he doing something to set her off?

Near the opposite end of town, he turned into a lane next to a white clapboard church and continued on past the parsonage to a small barn behind it. Two apple trees in the yard had leafed out since he was home last, and even in the falling moonlight, his mother's roses looked about to bloom. Livvy reached back for the satchel. Whit stopped at the barn, jumped down, and offered his hand. She took it with a quiet thank-you and stepped to the ground. When he didn't let go of her fingers, she looked up at him with the old challenge.

Her hair caught the moon and shimmered nearly white. Without thinking, he touched it lightly with his free hand. Her breath hitched.

If he kissed her, she'd either slap him or kick him or, worse yet, despise him. He ached.

"Thank you for coming with me."

She didn't pull away. Her challenging glare softened and her lips parted. Could she tell he was looking at them? He forced his eyes back to hers and let go of her hand. "I couldn't have gotten him here safely without your help."

She looked away—the second time that night, and the second time in her life that she'd not won a stare-down between them. "I couldn't let him lie there alone, bouncing all the way into town." She wrapped her arms around the satchel and held it against her chest like a barrier between them.

Softer, as if admitting a secret sin, "I couldn't let you go alone."

His knees nearly buckled and he shifted his weight to hide the fact. If he looked her in the eye he was liable to haul off and do something uncalled for. Instead, he focused on the shadowed row of columbines his mother had transplanted against the back porch.

"They usually leave the door unlocked. Let's go see."

Without another word, Livvy strode toward the parsonage and up the porch steps.

He'd done it again. He just didn't know what.

Breathe, Livvy, breathe. Fine thing it would be to faint and have Whit carrying her into his parents' parlor. She gripped the satchel and stood stock-still in the Huttons' small kitchen. Whit lit a lamp, set it on the table and pulled a chair out for her.

"Have a seat and I'll go check on the spare room."

"And who are you talking to down there, Whitaker Hutton?" His mother descended the stairs holding a kerosene lamp and clutching a wrapper to her chest. "Oh, Livvy. Welcome."

A sense of home swept into the room with Annie Hutton's warm smile and welcoming arm around Livvy's shoulders. "Whatever brings you to town this late at night?" A swift alarm crossed her face and she challenged her son with a mother's scowl.

Whit had already removed his hat and was hanging it on a peg by the door. "Tad Overton got himself shot up on the railbed in the canyon. His ma brought him to Baker's, and Livvy helped me haul him to Doc Mason's. We just finished there."

He took a seat at the table and heaved a great sigh. He was weary at best, and Livvy's arms longed to hold him.

Hold him? Heat rushed up her neck and she prayed Mrs. Hutton wouldn't notice in the dim lamp light.

"What a dear you are, Livvy. The boy's in good care at Doc's, but you must be beyond tired. Come with me and I'll show you to our spare room."

Livvy glanced at Whit and he gave her a brief nod. Fatigue and the last vestiges of worry made him look older. Twenty or more. She must look a sight herself.

Mrs. Hutton had already mounted the stairs and Livvy followed. At the landing, Whit's mother turned to the right and pushed open a door. From the room across the way a muffled flutter rose. Livvy smiled to herself. The pastor snored.

But so did her father. Maybe it came with the calling.

"Thank you, Mrs. Hutton. I—"

"Please, call me Annie. It's bad enough everyone in town still calls me Mrs. Hutton, even after all these years. Makes me feel old." She set the lamp on a table beside the bed, turned back a beautiful quilt and fluffed the pillow.

"Thank you, Annie. I do appreciate this, with no notice or anything."

Annie folded her arms against her wrapper and tipped her head to the side. "How long has it been since you and your folks visited? Three years? You've grown up quite a bit since the last time I saw you at a church picnic." She took Livvy's satchel and set it on a trunk at the foot of the bed. "You helped my Whit and rode all that way in a rough buckboard. You are a dear for doing such an unselfish thing and I am more than happy to let you rest here tonight."

"Thank you, again. You are very kind."

"I'll fetch you some warm water in the morning. I imagine you're too tired tonight to bathe."

Livvy dropped to the bed and hiked up her skirt to remove her boots. She hadn't realized how her back and feet ached until she sank into the soft feather ticking.

"This was Whit's room when he lived here," Annie said, looking around at the furniture. "I've tried to do it up a bit nicer so it's not so boyish. I hope it suits you."

Livvy gulped an unladylike breath and glanced at her host. "It's lovely." She smoothed a wrinkle in the eight-point star quilt. "Did you make this yourself?"

Annie smiled through a yawn. "Yes—pardon me!— years ago. It's an older one, but I love the bright red stars. So did Whit when he was a boy." She turned for the door and paused there. "You sleep as long as you want. I'll keep a plate warm for your breakfast." With that, she softly closed the door behind her.

Whit's bedroom. Whit's bed. Whit's longing look in the moonlight. Livvy warmed at the memory as she stepped out of her dress and simple petticoat. This was probably a completely different bed. Surely the ticking and pillow had not been his. But the quilt?

She slipped beneath the covers. The man muddled her mind. One minute he was a childish tease and the next a perfect, caring gentleman. How could he be both and stir such opposing reactions in her stomach—yearning and anger?

She'd think about all that tomorrow. Right now all she wanted was to lie back and surrender to slumber's long arms. She pulled the quilt higher, tucked it under her chin, and let out a sigh of her own.

Livvy tucked her legs up and snuggled deeper into the feather ticking, away from a teasing light. She squinted one eye open, gasped and bolted upright. An unfamiliar room, a strange bed. Her gaze landed on her satchel, traveled to the quilt and the four bright red stars that topped the bed. Her shoulders relaxed and she remembered. Whit's bed.

Whit's bed? She clutched the quilt to her throat and looked around the room. No sign of anyone but her. Bright sunlight poured in the window—it must be midmorning. She tossed the covers aside.

At the washstand, warm water greeted her fingers and she smiled at Annie Hutton's thoughtfulness. If Livvy couldn't have clean clothes, at least she could have a freshened body.

In no time she was booted, buttoned and combed out. She stood before the mirror and pulled her hair over her shoulder, plaiting it into a long braid. She twisted it low on her neck and pinned it in place, wanting instead to let it hang down her back on the ride home.

The thought fanned a tiny flame in her stomach and she turned to look at the quilt. Quickly she straightened it, propped up the pillow, gathered her satchel and rushed into the hall. The sooner she was out of Whit Hutton's bedroom, the better.

A door at the landing's end stood open, one she had not noticed the night before. Another fine quilt topped a bed there and a china-faced doll perched against a pink pillow. Whit's sister's room. The girl was two or three years younger, if Livvy remembered correctly. She must be about fifteen now.

Women's voices drew her to the stairway, and she hurried down and into the kitchen. A grown-up Martha Mae Hutton stood next to her mother at the counter, her bronze-colored hair as vivid as Livvy remembered. The homey scent of yeast-laced dough veiled the room. Both women turned at Livvy's arrival.

"Good morning!" Annie rubbed her hands against her apron and met Livvy with a brief hug. "I hope you slept well. You seemed to be when I slipped in earlier with the hot water."

Livvy ducked her head at being caught asleep so late. "Thank you. I—I don't usually sleep so long."

"Nothing to worry about." Annie brushed away Livvy's remark and returned to her work. "You do remember Martha, don't you? Marti, this is Ruth and Hubert Baker's granddaughter, Olivia Hartman."

A smile as warm as her mother's and terrifyingly close to her brother's spread across the girl's face. She extended her hand. "It's nice to see you again, Olivia. I think the last time was at the church picnic three or four years ago."

"Livvy, please. Call me Livvy." She took the girl's warm hand, smooth with flour. "Looks like I caught you in the middle of baking."

Marti pulled a plate from the warmer and set it at the kitchen table. "This is for you. We barely had enough to hold for you after Daddy and Whit finished breakfast. My brother eats like a horse now that he's up at your grand-father's place."

"Shame, Marti." Annie poured coffee, set the cup before Livvy and bumped her daughter with her hip, a playful move that forced a laugh from Livvy.

Marti lightly bumped her mother in return. "I'm not being mean, Mama. Just speaking the truth, that's all."

A bank of windows topped the counter and sink all along the west wall, and bright yellow curtains drew back at each end, matching the checked cloth on the table. Livvy seated herself and whispered a quick prayer over the eggs and bacon and biscuit. She was hungrier than she'd thought. "It's not often lately that I eat something I haven't cooked myself. This looks—and smells—wonderful."

The back door opened and Whit stepped in on the cheerful exchange. "You ready?" His question landed on Livvy's plate like a blob of cold grease. She looked at him, at her plate, and back to his creased brow.

"I need to get back to the ranch."

Chapter 6

"Stop fussing, Whit, and sit down and have some coffee." His mother didn't give Livvy a chance to answer before bringing two cups and the coffeepot to the table. "We've hardly had a good visit and here you want to rush off already. Can't you stay for dinner?"

She filled the cups, returned the pot to the stove and took a seat across the table. Her mischievous smile reminded Whit that no other preacher's kids could have had it as good as he and Marti did growing up.

He hung his hat on the chair back rather than the peg by the door. He and Livvy were not staying. This wasn't a social call, and he had calves to brand. Lord knew the trouble Buck and Jody Perkins could wrangle before he returned.

But the hungry look in Livvy's blue eyes set him back. It wasn't eggs and biscuits she was longing for. His impatience settled and he scooted to the table, gentled his voice. "Go ahead and eat, Livvy. We have time."

His mother cocked an eyebrow in that way she had.

Made him want to duck every time. She could always tell what he was thinking. He raised the heavy mug to his lips and sipped the black brew. Good cowboy coffee. Amazing what a delicate little preacher's wife could concoct.

"Did you check on Tad?" Livvy spread apple butter on a biscuit and looked at him as she took a bite.

He waited. Surprise lit her eyes and she turned to his mother. "This is wonderful, Mrs. Hu—Annie. I'd love to get your recipe."

Livvy couldn't have said anything better.

His mother beamed. "You'll have to come down this fall when Marti and I pick apples and you can make a batch with us." She slid Whit a bold look. "Of course, we'd love to see you before then, too."

He cleared his throat and swirled his coffee even though he had no sugar or cream in it to swirl. He was definitely outnumbered in the kitchen with three women, though Marti hadn't lit into him yet. She plopped a mound of dough in a crockery bowl, covered it with a towel and then poured herself some coffee. Taking a chair, she tossed her red curls, her long-standing attempt at appearing casual.

"So, is this Tad you speak of Tad Overton?" Marti spooned sugar into her coffee and added a cow's worth of cream.

"Yes," Livvy said, finishing her eggs. "Do you know him?"

Whit stiffened.

Marti turned her coffee mug around so the handle was on the left side. "We went to school together before he and his folks moved to Eight Mile." A slight blush colored her cheeks.

"He's a no-account fool."

Whit's comment deepened the blush. Marti speared him with a withering glare.

"What an unkind thing to say, Whit." His ma's reprimand didn't carry her usual fire. It didn't need to. Marti's ire heated the room.

Whit gulped his coffee, waited for his throat to stop burning. "He had no business getting mixed up in the train war. Now he's got himself shot and his mother will have to do all the chores until he heals up. Not only that, he took me away from the roundup, and the Perkins brothers are sitting on their thumbs at the ranch waiting for me to get back." He drained the cup. "At least they better be."

Livvy's eyes rounded as if she'd never seen him before.

His ma frowned. "Maybe one of them can help Mrs. Overton until Tad is well enough."

Whit shot her a glance. "They're doin' that, too."

Livvy stood and took her plate to the sink. "I'd be glad to help you clean up."

"Thank you, but you are in a hurry and we are not." His ma went into a small room off the kitchen and came back with two jars. She tied them into a dish towel and gave them to Livvy.

"Take these with you. If you don't serve it every meal to those hungry cowboys, it might last you a couple of weeks before you and Whit get back down." She snagged Whit with a motherly smile that hobbled him to a commitment.

Livvy hugged her. "Thank you again for letting us stay on such short notice."

"Think nothing of it, dear. This is home, you know."

No surprise to Whit that his ma embraced Livvy with her hospitality. Maybe someday Livvy would share more than the apple butter recipe, but they'd best be on their way before Marti busted a cinch. He chanced a sidelong look her way. She had a tight rein on her coffee and was still scowling.

He grabbed his hat off the chair and Livvy's cloak from a peg, then opened the door and stepped back for her to exit. Beneath his brim he peeked at his mother and caught her approving look. He had to get back to Eight Mile before all these women got him so flustered he didn't know bronc from broke.

"I'll tell your father you'll be back down after branding."

How could he argue with that? "Thanks for breakfast. And the apple butter." He planted a kiss on her cheek and looked over her shoulder through the open kitchen door. Marti stuck her tongue out at him.

His ma patted his cheek and leaned closer. "She's a real sweet girl, Whit."

He met her eyes for a moment—like looking in a mirror—but held his thoughts in check.

"Oh, Whit, look. Columbines." Livvy fingered the lavender fringe on the lush green border beneath the porch. "They're just like those we saw near the corrals."

"Aren't they lovely?" His ma descended the steps and stooped beside Livvy. "Caleb helped me dig these from the hills and transplant them our first spring here in the parsonage. I was in the family way with Whit at the time."

Embarrassed by his mother's casual reference to such a subject, he made for the wagon. Bess stood patiently where he'd left her an hour ago, dozing in the traces. Livvy followed and gathered her skirts. He offered his hand. She took it without hesitation and climbed into the seat. He joined her, tipped his hat to his ma, and turned Bess in the yard and up the lane.

Livvy set her satchel on the bench between herself and Whit. She'd have liked to spend the day with Annie and Marti comparing recipes, discussing flowers, even helping them with the bread. But she understood Whit's insistence that they get back to the ranch. Pop needed them both. Promising herself she'd return to Cañon City as soon as the apple butter ran out, she focused on the busy Main Street.

How much it had changed since she and her parents last visited. Or maybe it was she who had changed, noticing more now than what a younger girl saw. A distinguished three-story hotel claimed an entire block with Fremont Bank in one corner. Meat markets, a haberdashery, several mercantiles, a drug store. The boardwalk appeared to be more even than she remembered, and ladies in fine clothes with parasols walked in groups or on gentlemen's arms.

She glanced down at her plain day dress. Not exactly what a young woman wore to town. She touched her twisted braid, suddenly aware that she'd not thought to bring a hat or bonnet. But this had not been a social visit. At least she didn't know anyone in town other than the Huttons. Slight balm for her sudden discomfort.

A man on horseback loped down the street, kicking up dust and pebbles. Empty freight wagons rumbled by, returning from the mining camps and on their way to the livery. Buggy wheels creaked, reins slapped, children hollered. Noise and movement rose around her like a blustery storm. During the last few weeks at Pop's, Livvy had grown accustomed to the serene mountain setting. She'd nearly forgotten the clutter and commotion of city life.

Pretending to look across the street, she peeked at Whit. His face was a study in stone. Unreadable. His jaw clenched so tight that a muscle bulged just below his ear. That should tell her something, but she didn't know what.

In all their growing-up days, she'd not seen him angry as he had been today when his sister mentioned Tad Overton. The girl was obviously fond of the young patient, and Livvy did not doubt that Marti might pay Tad a visit while he recuperated at Doc Mason's.

Well, Whit better not find out about it. For a moment she was glad she didn't have a brother telling her what to do. Not that Whit wouldn't try the same tactic on her. But she didn't see him as a brother.

What *did* she see him as? Her pulse jumped into rhythm with Bess's pace. Livvy took a deep breath and peered past her bench partner and through the trees across the river. She caught the top of the Hot Springs Bath House before Whit took the curve at the west end of town.

Bess slowed as she pulled the wagon up the gently sloping road. Whit relaxed. He'd been tense the entire time they were in Cañon City—except for last night when he'd thanked her for coming with him. Her insides warmed at the memory. And he hadn't teased her once, not that she missed it, but it was so uncharacteristic. Was she getting a glimpse into what he was like as a man?

And man he was, of that she was keenly aware. His legs stretched a good three inches past hers where they sat on the bench, and his hands were sure with the reins, callused and tanned. Strong, yet gentle, too. She smoothed back her hair where he had touched it the night before.

He looked at her. She jerked her hand down, tucked it into the folds of her skirt.

"You thinking about something?" The familiar smirk tipped his mouth.

So much for the grown-up Whit.

She straightened, pressing her spine against the hard seat back. "And exactly what should I be thinking about?"

He huffed, made that scoffing sound in his throat that she hated. The vision of his tenderness splintered.

She looked to her right, followed the jagged skyline that sliced high above the road. A rock-layer rainbow of ocher and red and green stepped down the abutment in wide bands. Such a history the stone must tell, if only she knew how to read it.

"Livvy."

She jumped at his strangled moan, doubting it was her name she'd heard. Which layer of temperament would he present this time?

He turned Bess off the road and pulled to a stop. The horse immediately bent her head to the bunch grass poking through the rocky landscape. Whit twisted halfway on the bench, pinning Livvy in place with dark, inscrutable eyes.

"What?" She lifted her chin, pressed her shoulders back.

"We're too old to carry on like children."

She breathed in through her nose. Breathed out. "Whatever do you mean?"

Whit's eyes had aged since driving Tad into town last night. The earlier smirk and his throaty huff were the only remaining vestiges of boyhood.

"You are like fire and ice."

She splashed him with a scalding look.

"See, that's just what I mean. One minute you are sweet and smooth as my mother's apple butter, the next you're as snorty and mean as an unbroke colt."

Livvy stiffened, stared straight ahead, focused on breathing. She clasped her hands in her lap and struggled to maintain her composure after being compared to a horse. A *horse.*

"Don't you think we should be on our way?"

He dropped the reins over the buckboard and leaned closer. "What I think is if we do not clear the air right now, I will leave you here beside the road."

Her head jerked around and his face was so close to hers that his breath washed over her lips. "You wouldn't."

One eyebrow reared. "Oh, but I would."

Angry tears marshaled in her throat and clawed their way upward. She dug her nails into her hands to distract her disloyal emotions. He could easily pick her up and toss her off the wagon. Or she could salvage her pride by stepping down voluntarily. Then he'd be forced to tell her grandfather that he was so rude and unkind she refused to ride home with him.

Clear the air, he'd said. She couldn't even clear her

thoughts. She drew in another deep breath. *Oh, Lord, give me words. Give me a way out. Give me—*

Peace. That's what Whit was demanding. Peace between them. Well, it took two to make peace and she had a few demands of her own. The realization strengthened her, calmed her quaking heart.

"Very well. Let us *clear the air,* as you put it." She turned to face him full-on, scooting back a bit to add a small distance between them. Thank goodness for the satchel. "You are not exactly the finest stallion in the herd, you know." Poor choice of words, but the first that came to mind.

His mouth twitched. He was laughing at her on the inside.

Her finger flew up like a pointed gun and she leveled it at his nose. "See what I mean? You laugh at me. You mock me. You treat me like I am an eight-year-old with freckles and pigtails."

"Sometimes you are." His mouth rippled, losing ground against the urge to grin.

"You are doing it right this minute."

"And so are you. You're acting like a child, all huff and hooves at the slightest little thing that isn't how you expect it to be. Life is not like that, Livvy. Life is full of badger holes and rockslides. You have to learn how to ride around them or ride through them and pray you don't break your neck."

"You pray?" Immediately she regretted the stinging words and covered her mouth as if she could stop the pain that shot across his face. "I'm sorry," she whispered. "I didn't mean that."

His eyes hardened into obsidian.

Bess stepped forward in her grazing and the wagon jerked. A hawk cried above them and some small creature in a hidden crevice sent pebbles trailing down the rock face. Livvy felt as heartless and cold as those tumbling stones.

At once she saw the truth in his earlier words—and hers; she'd not deny them. But he was right. She was not living as she'd been raised. And how long had it been since *she* had truly prayed, set her desires out before the Lord and asked for His guidance?

She laid her hand on Whit's arm. "Please, forgive me."

His eyes softened—slightly—but his lips and his muscled arm remained a hard defense.

"You are right. I am fire and ice." She withdrew her hand. "But so are you. You can be tender and caring and turn right around and tease me in the next breath. I don't like it."

He scanned the ridge above them, worked his jaw, squinted as if peering into the deepest fissures.

"I'll work on it." The words chipped out like flint, but his gaze returned to her face and he reached for her hand, swallowed it with his own. "Truce?"

He'd asked this once before, in the meadow. His eyes had pleaded once before, last night behind the parsonage. She had granted him the slack her grandfather spoke of and then yanked it back. Unyielding. Unbending. Unforgiving.

His rough hands warmed her, promised protection, help. She'd rather have him as a friend than an enemy. "Truce."

Chapter 7

The air wasn't exactly clear, but it was tolerable. Whit wanted clean and pure, like the morning after a summer rain. Instead he got cloudy and rushing, like Wilson Creek after a gully washer. But at least the water was flowing.

At least there was water.

He turned Bess back into the road and flicked the ribbons against her rump. She clopped onto the hardened surface and the wagon wheels found their way into the ruts. Livvy sat more relaxed beside him, as if spent after her storm. He felt the same.

Her comment about prayer bit the hardest, most likely because it was true. He had pretty much followed his own head, not asked the Lord what he should be doing. The family wanted him to take over the mercantile and his pa had hinted at college. But the idea of books and papers and professors made him want to kick and buck. He'd never be a preacher or any other kind of man who made his living indoors. Ever since that first summer he'd worked for Hubert Baker during roundup, he'd wanted to cowboy, learn to ranch, someday own his own spread.

It was *in* him.

His ma had often talked about his father having a way with horses. Whit believed he had the same, plus a good head for cows.

He'd even sketched out a brand: an H beneath an inverted V like a mountain peak. He planned to register it as soon as he got a chance.

Today would have been the chance if not for Baker and the Perkins boys waiting on his return. He'd have to make another trip to town, an event sure to please the preacher's wife. A smile tugged at his lips.

She liked Livvy. So did he. But he had to get that hump out of Livvy's back before they could get along—just like a green-broke colt. They had to come to an understanding.

It took every ounce of grit he had not to look at her sitting beside him, all sweet-smelling and proper. And even more not to toss that satchel in the back, reach around her waist and pull her closer. She'd sure enough scared the fire out of him when she didn't even flinch at his threat to leave her behind. He'd thought she was gonna call his bluff and jump right off the wagon. But he'd been right in his guess about what set her off—his teasing. He had to break that habit or get her to see it was all in good fun.

He huffed. As fun as Oro crow-hopping across the corral after Whit stuck his spurs to him. A lesson learned.

By the time Bess made the turnoff to the ranch road, she'd kicked up her pace. Knowing that home lay ahead, she took to it on her own without Whit's coaxing, but he kept her speed in check. He didn't want her running at it as she had on the way to town. They'd nearly rattled the buckboard apart. He could feel the give in the seat and hear a few extra knocks. He'd check it out when they reached the ranch, make sure the under rigging was still in good shape.

Livvy wiped her forehead with the back of her hand. Unlike him, she had no hat to shield her eyes or protect her pale skin from the sun. Would she take his if he offered?

He'd better not press his luck.

They'd left last night in such a hurry that she hadn't brought a bonnet. She'd thought only about Tad and him, not herself. A warm spot spread in his belly like a hot meal on a cold night. He could get used to that.

"You acted like you knew what you were doing last night." He slid her a glance, hoping she'd know that was a compliment.

"Doc Patterson's place is next door to ours. I've helped him some." She turned her hands palm up and studied them a moment. "He tried to get me to go to nursing school. Said I had the touch. But I don't want to be a full-time nurse."

"What *do* you want to do?"

Her fingers curled and she turned her head toward the ridgeline that snaked around the valley and flattened into bluffs at the end. "The same thing most women want, I suppose."

He chuckled. "Pretty dresses and a bunch of beaux calling?"

She huffed and shot him a warning look.

He waited for the steam to burn off and tried again. "A big spread in the high parks and cow-calf pairs as far as the eye can see?"

This time she didn't look at him, kept her eyes straight ahead. Had he said the wrong thing already?

"That sounds rather nice."

Her soft answer sent a jolt through him that bounced off his ribs and then settled easy on his heart.

"You do work for my grandfather, you know." Her voice strengthened. "My mother grew up here, and I learned to ride here. It's not like I don't know my way around livestock."

He couldn't argue with that. Didn't want to argue with that. Maybe he could fit a pair of *H*s beneath that mountain peak brand. But he was getting way ahead of himself.

The ranch road skirted the creek bottom, leaving the thick, deep grass unmarred by wagon wheels and horse hooves. He spotted several head he could have easily pushed to the corrals. They watched the buckboard without reaction.

Livvy broke the silence. "Why were you so mad at your sister?"

If Olivia Hutton could jump a maverick steer as quick as she asked a straight question, he'd have her riding on the roundup.

"What makes you think I'm mad at her?"

Livvy branded him with a blue glare. "Now who's playing games?"

He frowned and flicked Bess into a hard trot. "She has no business getting tangled up with Tad Overton. He's not to be trusted."

"How do you know?"

Whit bristled against her push into his family's personal affairs. A final turn into the main yard and he stopped Bess at the house. "I just do."

Livvy snickered under her breath. Pretty pleased with herself, she was, as she snatched up the satchel and her wrap and then held him with a taunting look. "Well?"

"Well, what?"

"Are you going to help me down or not?"

He clamped his teeth, wrapped the reins around the brake handle and jumped down.

Infuriating woman.

He handed her down and watched her stop at the purple bush by the front door and bury her face in it before going inside. She didn't look behind her, just stepped through the door and closed it.

But she did not slam it. He reset his hat, took up the reins and clucked Bess to the barn. A skittish hope danced around him and the future began to unfurl itself.

While he unhitched Bess and brushed her down, he calculated how much money he'd saved and considered asking Baker if he could run a few of his own cows in with the ranch herd. But he needed to register a brand first.

Next trip, he promised himself, pleased at the prospect of doing business as well as visiting his family. Two birds with one stone. Yes, the future was looking better all the time. He opened the pasture gate behind the barn, led Bess through and pulled off her bridle. As he closed the gate he scanned the green bottomland for the other horses Baker kept close. There should be six. He counted three, including Bess.

He strode to the barn and pushed open the tack room door. Baker's saddle and tack were gone. So were Buck's and Jody's. Whit jerked his hat off, slapped it on his leg and shoved it back on. He grabbed his outfit and took it to the pasture, where he hung his saddle and blanket on the fence and whistled for Oro.

The gelding raised his head and looked Whit's way. His tawny coat gleamed against the meadow's green, and he trotted to the fence and greeted Whit with a deep-chested rumble.

"You saw them leave, didn't you?" Whit mumbled his complaint to the horse as he bridled and saddled him. Then he swung into the saddle, rode through the gate, latched it and headed for the farthest canyon. "Let's go find them."

Delores Overton was gone. Livvy looked in the bedrooms, the parlor, Pop's study, the dining room and kitchen, even the root cellar out back, though no reason came to mind for the woman to be there. She returned to the kitchen for the egg basket and scrap can and went out to the garden and coop. No Delores.

And no Pop.

She hushed her rampant thoughts. Pop often went for a ride to look things over. Surely he was fine. Out counting his cows. Hopefully not every single one this afternoon. That's what he had Whit and Buck and Jody for.

She tossed the scraps and entered the coop while the chickens fought over the best pieces. Fourteen eggs this morning, or rather afternoon. Enough to bake a pound cake and have a few to boil. She could almost taste Annie Hutton's apple butter melting into a golden slice of warm cake. Her mouth watered.

Buck and Jody would make quick work of the fruity spread. Where were those boys, anyway? It was too late in the day to be at Overton's doing chores. And there was enough to be done around here to keep them busy all summer besides gathering cattle. The fence around the garden plot needed mending, and the woodpile shrank a little every day.

She hooked the basket on her arm, shielded her eyes against the westerly sun and looked out to the pasture, counted the horses. Her chest tightened as she scoured the green meadow for a buckskin and her grandfather's stocky gray. Bess and another dark horse grazed unhurriedly. No gray. Delores Overton wasn't the only one missing.

She and Whit hadn't been home a half hour and already he was gone.

She hurried from the coop, careful to latch the gate. She didn't need coyotes nosing their way in due to her carelessness. With the egg basket on her arm, she hiked her skirts and ran to the house. Where was everyone?

The kitchen hugged the north edge of the ranch house, shaded behind a big pine on the west end and therefore cooler than any other room in the summer. But not bright like the Huttons'. How cheerful yellow curtains would be against the dark wood walls.

She washed the eggs and laid them out on a tea towel as her earlier words floated by with tempting appeal.

I learned to ride here.

And she'd done it without a side saddle. No place for such a contraption on a cattle spread. She shuddered. How could you keep your seat chasing cows without two feet in the stirrups?

Everyone had ridden astride, even her mother and Mama Ruth. The three of them had often trailed up to the bluffs, where they sat gazing down at the creek bottom and the ranch buildings.

Dusty memories of horseflesh and leather lured her to her grandfather's bedroom, where she knelt before the chest by the door. She had long since outgrown her riding skirt, but Mama Ruth had worn denims. Said she didn't care what her highfalutin English relatives thought. This was Colorado and she'd do as she pleased. Livvy warmed with the tender ache the memory pressed.

She lifted the lid on the trunk and tipped it back against the wall. Then she carefully dug through the linens and dresses that had been Mama Ruth's. Pausing, she leaned out and looked into the dining room. Heaven forbid that Pop come in and find her snooping. Maybe she should wait and ask his permission. Would he allow what she was thinking?

Determined, she returned to her search and found what she wanted at the trunk's bottom. Denims, just like Whit and Pop wore, only smaller. A boy's size—her grandmother's size. Livvy stood and held them at her waist. Looking at herself in the glass over Mama Ruth's dressing table, she pulled a lopsided grin. With a hat and her hair tucked up, she could pass for a hired hand.

Excitement burned through her veins like a fast fuse.

She returned everything else to its neat order and closed the trunk. Then she *borrowed* one of Pop's old work hats from the back of a bentwood rack in the corner, clutched the denims to her chest and ran to her room.

Quietly she closed her door and laid the pants across the brass footboard. She caught the movement in the glass across the room and looked up. Her cheeks were flushed, her eyes wide with anticipation. She shoved the hat on her head and pulled it forward, low over her right eye like Whit wore his. Perfect. But she'd have to line the hatband with newsprint to keep the old Stetson from flying off.

The back door closed.

Livvy choked and snatched off the hat. She rolled the denims and shoved them under the bed. The hat followed, and she fluffed out the dust ruffle. Did it always stick out or should it be kicked back a little?

She licked both palms and smoothed her mussed hair on the sides, giggling at the childish tactic. She hadn't done that in years.

She straightened her skirt, opened the door and walked as elegantly as possible into the dining room toward the kitchen. No other sounds had followed the door's closing. She had no idea who had entered.

At the doorway she stopped.

He sat at the work table beneath the kitchen window, his hat lying next to his propped elbows. He braced his head in both hands and his fingers gripped his dark hair. He looked so—so *alone*.

She ached to reach out to him, to be a comfort, a companion. But they were only beginning to be friends, working out their stubborn differences, working together on her grandfather's ranch. Nothing more.

He raised his head and looked straight into her eyes. And in a breath she knew that Whit Hutton could see into her very soul.

Chapter 8

Whit stared at Livvy standing in the doorway, her lips parted as if to speak. If he wasn't so angry, he'd kiss her soundly. As it was, his own heart hammered in his head and it had nothing to do with courting.

"Jody's gone."

"Gone?" Livvy's brow wrinkled and she came to the table. "What about Pop and Buck? Are they okay? Is Pop all right?"

Of course she'd worry for her grandfather. He should have mentioned Baker first. He smoothed his hair back. The knots in his shoulders tightened. "Your grandfather is fine. He and Buck are out in the barn unsaddling their horses."

Visibly relieved, Livvy went to the stove and opened the flue. "I'll make some coffee."

She pumped water into the coffeepot and set it over the fire. He watched mutely as she scooped out beans and added them to the mill. The grinding matched his churning thoughts, but the aroma soothed him. Maybe that was all he needed. Hot, strong coffee.

His stomach growled. Livvy smiled and threw him a sidelong glance. "I know you had eggs this morning, but that's all I've got. Want some to go with the coffee?"

He blew out a heavy breath, rolled his shoulders and leaned back in the chair. "That sounds good."

He'd not watched a woman work—work for his comfort— for any length of time. It touched something inside him, brought to mind the way his father watched his mother.

Livvy moved smoothly between tasks, wasting no effort. He rubbed the stiffness in his neck and studied her mannerisms, the soft curves in her dress, the hair working loose from her coiled braid.

She added the ground coffee to the pot and more wood to the stove. Then she spooned bacon grease in an iron skillet and gathered four eggs from the counter's far corner. At the cabinet she drew out a loaf of bread, cut two thick slices and laid one on each of two plates.

He could get used to this setup, sitting in the kitchen, enjoying female company. Livvy's company. "You going to share that apple butter with me?"

He winced at his tone. He needed to work on talking with her. He couldn't seem to say anything that wasn't a borderline jab.

But she must have been worried about Baker, because she didn't goad him back or get all worked up.

"No, I am not. I'm saving it to have with pound cake. You will have to wait." She buttered the bread and set his plate before him, then started breaking the eggs into the skillet.

"Thank you." He bit off the corner. "But I don't smell pound cake."

Her cheeks colored. Couldn't be the stove—she'd just stirred the fire.

"I haven't gotten to it yet." She pushed at the escaping hair. "I had other things to do when we got back." She fingered the same strands again and looked around as if searching for something. "Gathered eggs, fed the chickens. Hunted for Mrs. Overton."

She looked at him then, worry clouding her eyes. "She's not here, either."

"I know. Buck said he sent Jody with her early this morning. She wanted to go home, and Jody took her so he could help with chores." Whit shoved the rest of the bread in his mouth and chewed the way he wanted to chew on the boy. "He never came back."

Livvy flipped the eggs over, the way he liked. She came to the table and retrieved his plate. "More bread?" She served the eggs with cracked peppercorns and paused at the counter, waiting for his answer.

He could look at her all day and never come up with the right words, so he nodded.

She added a fork to his plate and set the food before him, then took the other chair.

He shoved his chair back. "I need to wash."

She stopped him with a hand on his. "It's all right." She hinted at a smile and scooted closer to the table. "Just don't tell Buck and Jody."

He chuckled. The day wasn't all bad. He was eating in private with Miss Olivia Hartman. Until the kitchen door banged open and Baker and Buck walked in.

Buck stopped, took one look at Livvy, then ran back out. Splashing sounds carried into the kitchen.

Baker pumped water at the sink, washed and dried his hands on a towel that Livvy kept on a nail for his use. His ranch, his house. He could wash wherever he pleased.

Livvy whisked away her plate and checked on the coffee. She added grease and several more eggs to the skillet, and soon offered two more plates filled with fried eggs and buttered bread. Baker brought two chairs from the dining room and motioned for Livvy to join them.

The coffee smelled ready and Livvy must have agreed, for she bunched her apron and brought the pot to the table. Baker set three stoneware mugs and a china cup and saucer on the smooth wood surface and took the farthest seat against the west wall with his right leg angled out from the table. He had a clear view of the kitchen, the window and the back door.

Buck joined them, as did Livvy. She lifted her brows at the mixed dishes on the table and eyed her grandfather.

Baker read her query. "In here I like a mug. Less formal. Your grandmother didn't mind."

"Makes the coffee better, I think." Buck shoveled into his eggs and Baker watched him fill his face. Withering under the close examination, the boy swallowed, laid his fork down and bowed his head.

Silence stood at the table as Baker gathered his thoughts. "Thank You, Lord, for this food and for bringing Livvy and Whit home safely. Thank You for bringing Tad and his mother here so we could help." He paused and cleared his throat. "Save him, Lord. Amen."

Baker sure enough knew how things stood. Whit wasn't sure if the saving had to do with Tad Overton's body or soul, but it really didn't matter. God always seemed to take both into account.

Livvy bit into her bread and sipped coffee from the teacup. What an old softy Pop was, knowing she liked the colorful china better than the heavy stoneware.

From the way Buck finished off his eggs, she wondered what the men and Mrs. Overton had had for breakfast. If they'd had anything. Livvy glanced at the pie safe, remembering last night's interrupted dessert. She had a second pie tucked away, if it hadn't disappeared, too.

"What did Doc Mason say about Tad?" Pop sheared off half his bread and gulped his coffee.

Whit shook his head in disgust, a signal Livvy recognized all too well. "He wants to keep him for a few days, keep an eye on him."

"Keep him out of trouble, more likely." Pop's bread disappeared beneath his silvery mustache and he chewed as if the bread were a week old and tough.

"I told Doc we'd take care of the bill. Can't see the widow havin' enough to pay for what her fool son did."

Buck studied his plate and kept his head down. The men stopped eating and stared at him. In the silence, the boy must have sensed their scrutiny, for he peeked out from under his pale brows and frowned.

"I know what you're thinkin'."

"And just what are we thinkin'?" Whit's eyes narrowed into skewers.

"That it's all my fault."

"How's that?" Pop said.

Buck cut a glance at Whit and blanched as if he'd seen a Ute warrior, spear in hand. "Whit said I was in charge and if anything went wrong he'd blame me."

Pop grunted, gulped another mouthful of coffee and eyed his foreman. "I was here, too. Can't be entirely your fault."

Color returned to Buck's face and he sat a little straighter.

"Though he is your brother, not mine."

Whit's lip quirked on one side and he picked up his coffee. "Where do you think he went after Overton's?" He held Buck with a you'd-better-tell-me stare.

Buck stalled.

The boy was about to become the next entrée and Livvy regretted having nothing else to feed the men. Gone one night, and here they were near starving. And now they'd cleaned out her eggs, too. She'd never get to sneak off and ride with a day's worth of baking and cooking ahead.

She picked up her dashed hopes and went to the pie safe.

Safe, indeed.

"He's a good boy," Buck said. "I'm sure he helped Mrs. Overton with her chores like I told him to."

"That's not what I asked you." Whit's eyes flicked a warning.

Livvy served Whit a fat piece of pie. "Look what I found."

He ignored her.

Buck fidgeted with his fork and then laid it on the table with a defeated sigh. "I think he went upriver toward Fort DeRemer at Texas Creek."

"Fort *what?*" Whit's expression hardened.

"DeRemer," Pop said. "Named after a man who fought in the Civil War. Just a rock wall, but the Denver and Rio Grande men are building them at strategic points along the river and firing on the Santa Fe workers. Heard about it when I was in town last week." He mumbled something into his coffee. "It's all gonna bust out like a full-bellied storm caught in a canyon."

Buck watched Livvy slice into the pie. "Jody wanted to hire on to lay track for the Santa Fe company. He ain't a good enough shot to hole up behind those rock forts with the Denver fellas. But I didn't think he was serious, 'specially since we got all them cows to gather and calves to brand."

Livvy's hand stopped above the pie as an idea sliced through her mind. Buck noticed and looked as if he wasn't going to get any of the juicy dessert. She caught herself, cut him a bigger piece and set it before him.

"Thank you, ma'am."

"You are welcome." At least the boy was learning something.

"I'll admit, we talked on it some," Buck said around a mouthful. "Fact is, Jody thought they'd want you for a hired gun, Whit, being's you're such a crack shot and all. Figured they'd be after you for sure since you know the country."

Whit's hand tightened around his fork and Livvy feared he might stab Buck right there in front of God and everybody. Instead he nailed the boy to his chair with an icy glare.

Pop snorted. "Whit's too smart for that, son. He knows which side his bread's buttered on."

Buck frowned but didn't ask and Livvy wasn't about to tell him what it meant. This was not her conversation. Plus she had something on her mind, which required all her concentration to frame exactly right, and now might be the perfect time to bring it up.

She served Pop and then herself and resumed her seat. A quarter of the pie remained.

"My guns are for snakes, coyotes and lions," Whit said. "Not taking potshots at men working on laying a railroad that we need through these mountains. Regardless whose name is on the train."

Pop grunted again. Seemed as though he did that more and more since Mama Ruth had been gone. She'd always insisted he speak in complete sentences.

"I'll ride over to Cunningham's early tomorrow." Whit pushed his plate back and looked at Pop. "See if their boys can help us with the branding."

"Won't be necessary." Pop leaned his arms on the table, tilted his head over his plate. "I can still ride. But I'd be more help on the ground. You and Buck can drive them off the mountain to the bunch grounds. You rope 'em, and Buck and I can hold 'em down."

"Who will brand?"

Pop cut a look at Livvy without raising his head.

Her breath stuck in her throat. Did her grandfather really have that much faith in her? Did he remember all those years she and her mother and Mama Ruth had horsebacked through these hills?

"No." Whit's jaw tightened and the muscle below his ear bulged.

Pop's gaze shifted to his foreman. "Are you questioning my judgment?"

Livvy pulled air through her nose. She watched the battle in Whit's eyes—his desire to please and respect his boss, and his apprehension at taking a woman on a roundup. He wouldn't meet her gaze and she was glad. She couldn't stand to have him look down on her.

But she wasn't going to sit quietly by and let them discuss her as if she wasn't there. "I can do it, Pop. Mama Ruth and Mother and I rode all over this ranch when I was growing up."

He smiled and his mustache quivered. "I know you did. They were good teachers. All the Baker women are good horsewomen. But it's the branding I want you to do. Do you think you can handle that?"

"Yes." And why not? She'd wrung chickens' necks and cleaned fish and patched up bloody men like Tad Overton. How hard could it be?

"You listen to what Whit tells you. He'll show you how on a couple and then turn it over to you."

He will? She slid a glance at Whit and saw the battle still raging. Not only was his boss taking over, he was telling him how to do his job and bringing a woman into the mix. She sat straighter. She would not disappoint him.

"You'll be needin' your grandmother's denims." Pop stood and picked up his plate.

Fear leaped up and Livvy followed it. "You're right. I know where they are." Should she have said that? "I'll get them from the trunk right now."

She dashed out of the kitchen, through the dining room and into Pop's bedroom. She opened the trunk for a moment, then dropped the lid and peeked around the doorframe. Chairs scraped against the kitchen floor. If she hurried she could make it to her room unseen.

How wicked she was, deceiving her grandfather into thinking she was pure and honest. Guilt sat heavy on her formerly light spirit. She must confess. But not yet. Not until after she proved that she could ride and brand as well as any cowhand on the ranches of Eight Mile Mountain.

And brand she would.

Chapter 9

The muscles in Whit's neck clamped like a farrier's clincher. His wild-hare comparison of Livvy jumping maverick steers was about to come to life. That was just what he needed—a girl and her crippled grandfather traipsing off into the thick brush. Blasted Jody Perkins. If Whit got his hands on him before the boy got himself shot, Perkins'd wish he'd never heard of the railroad.

Livvy had lit out of the kitchen like a jackrabbit in tall grass. He took his plate and cup to the sink and told Buck to do the same. Baker had already gone to the barn.

What happened to the peaceful afternoon of watching a beautiful woman do what she was good at? Now he had to spend three or four days watching her do what she'd never done before.

It could be worse. But not much.

Riding leisurely along smooth trails and open meadows was not even close to chasing a wild cow without getting hooked. Or breaking a horse's leg in a badger hole.

Or getting raked off the saddle in thick timber. Lord have mercy on them all.

As he reached for his hat, she returned to the kitchen. Her cheeks were flushed and she was near bustin' with excitement. He didn't need excitement. He needed levelheaded cow sense, a strong back and a sure hand. He looked at her hands.

"I thought you were gone." She pumped water into a dishpan, then set it on the stove before pulling out the flour bin.

He left his hat on the chair back, spread his feet squarely beneath him, and crossed his arms at his chest. "Do you have gloves?"

The question stopped her forward motion. "Excuse me?"

"Gloves. You know, those things you put on your hands." Irritation called up the worst in him and he almost regretted the sarcasm.

She planted her fists on her hips, faced him and raised her chin. "What has your back up, Mr. Hutton? Or do you not like the idea of a woman on roundup?"

He stood his ground. "What I don't like is you dodging my question."

"Hmm." She turned to the counter and set out a large crockery bowl. "Let me see now—I have some lovely pine-green gloves I wear with my traveling suit, white gloves I save for church and a very nice pair of kid-leather gloves for riding." With a tin cup she scooped flour from the bin into the bowl. "Yes, I have gloves."

Whit's neck muscles knotted. This was exactly what he didn't need.

In two strides he was beside her and grabbed her hand, relieving it of the cup. He forced her fingers against his own, palm to palm. Hardened and rough, his fingers topped hers by two knuckles.

He leaned in. "Feel that?" He pressed her hand between both of his. The racing pulse in her bare wrist beat against his arm, and her eyes widened with surprise. "Feel those calluses? The hard cracked skin? Is that what you want for yourself?"

She didn't pull away. Just stared at their hands flattened against each other like two hotcake griddles.

He dropped her hand. "Your nice kid leather won't last through one morning. And neither will your skin without work gloves. You'll be branded as sure as the calves Baker is so all-fired certain you can handle."

"I know that. I have watched brandings."

"Watching is not the same as doing."

An internal fire flared her eyes to sapphires, and the flame jumped to his heart like a wild ember. Anger or protectiveness—he didn't know which pressed him harder, but either one would cloud his judgment and he could not afford that. He took a step back, grabbed his hat off the chair and shoved it on with a stony stare.

"I am sure Pop has something I can use." Her hands balled around her bunched apron and her chin hitched up. He'd seen that same determination in old steers on the fight.

He huffed out a hot breath. Why had he tried to scare her off? She was determined to go.

"We leave at sunup."

He slammed the door on his way out. Infuriating woman.

He stormed to the bunkhouse and dug through his few extra clothes and tack until he found the gloves he'd worn when he started for Baker four years ago. He'd grown a mite since then. Like skunk cabbage in a wet summer, his pa had said.

He held one against his hand and his fingers topped the glove by two knuckles. No holes. Stiff, but still good protection. They'd do. He shoved them under his bedroll and headed for the barn. He needed to plan a strategy with Baker.

Livvy dragged in air and braced herself against the counter. Whitaker Hutton had more gall than any man she had ever known. How dare he compare the two of them? Why, that was like comparing gingham and leather. She looked at the hand he'd held, felt again the heat in his fingers and the way it made her heart pound.

No, that wasn't it at all. He'd simply taken her by surprise. Caught her off guard the way he always did. What happened to their short-lived truce? Why couldn't he let her be who she was? *Accept* her for who she was.

She mixed yeast and warm water in a small bowl and set it aside. Then she carried the now-boiling dishpan to the sink, dunked the day's dishes and shaved in a few soap curls with a paring knife.

After washing the dishes, she turned to baking bread—the perfect activity for taking out her frustration. Adding flour by the cupful, she worked the dough into a sizable mound, punching out the air and knots, picturing Whit as she kneaded.

Her mind played with the word and brought up *needed*. Humph. She pounded the dough again, tucked it under into a smooth ball and threw it in the bread bowl to rise. She needed Whit Hutton like she needed a third leg.

The afternoon flew by with baking and packing plates and flatware in an old flour sack she planned to tie on her saddle horn. After considering the clanking of tin against her horse's shoulder, she unpacked everything. Instead she'd get up early and slice meat and bread and stack it together. The men could eat with their hands. So could she.

They weren't taking a wagon. No lemonade. Surely

Pop had an extra canteen. She'd rather die of thirst than ask Whit for one.

Working the Bar-HB and the fringes of neighboring ranches for strays, they'd be back each night to sleep. As happy as she was about riding with the men, she knew she'd be dog tired at day's end. She also knew the others depended on her to keep them fed.

She put a roast in the Dutch oven, added water, salt, pepper, onions and the lid, and shoved it to the back of the oven to cook overnight. Then she went to her bedroom to prepare for tomorrow. She still needed to fit the hat and find a blouse or shirtwaist to wear with Mama Ruth's denims. Maybe Pop had an old shirt she could borrow. And gloves, too. She rubbed her hands together, recalling Whit's rough forcefulness—so unlike that day in the columbines.

At least she'd had enough sense to bring her own boots for summer on the ranch.

She took the hat to her grandfather's study, where she found a stack of old *Cañon City Times* newspapers he kept for fire starters in the winter. She pulled one from the bottom and a headline caught her eye. Tucking a leg beneath her, she settled into the leather-covered desk chair to read.

The United States Supreme Court on April 21 granted the primary right of way through the narrow gorge above Cañon City to the Denver & Rio Grande Western Railroad. The ruling should put to rest the ongoing Royal Gorge Railroad War between D&RG and the Atchison, Topeka and Santa Fe Railway.

Livvy let the paper flop back. The article was nearly two months old. If the Supreme Court had ruled, then why were Santa Fe crews laying track? No wonder the Denver men were sabotaging the rail. But must they shoot at mere boys like Tad Overton?

She spread the paper across her grandfather's desk and folded back the edge. Then she turned the broadsheet over and folded the new edge back, continuing to alternate the folds front and back until she had a large fanlike strip. She pressed the folds together and flattened them, then tucked the strip under the sweatband inside the old hat. *John B. Stetson* was stamped into the leather in gold letters. She tried it on and it slid down over her eyes.

Tipping it back, she looked through the stack for other interesting stories.

"School Superintendent Unearths More Fossil Remains." Livvy shuddered. Who wants to go around digging up old dead animals on purpose?

She folded the sheet into a long fan, and three pages later, her grandfather's Stetson stayed put. She rose to go look in her mirror and stopped short. Whit leaned inside the doorway, arms folded against his chest and one booted foot crossed over the other.

She jerked off the hat. "How long have you been standing there?"

"Long enough to know you look like a toadstool with that thing on."

Hot blood rushed into her face and she clenched her jaw. He'd better be on his horse when she got that stamp iron in her hands.

Uninvited, he sauntered to the desk, picked up the hat and shoved it back on her head. She couldn't move. Nor could she see him, he stood so tall above her and so close. Mindful of her tendencies, she focused on breathing through her nose.

He bent to the side and peeked under the brim. A distinct ripple twisted his mouth. He straightened and shoved the hat down farther until it pinched her ears. "You want it screwed down good and tight so it doesn't fly off if you get to running."

She hated him, yet she could not make her feet walk away from the desk.

He snorted like the horse that he was and she refused to raise her head to look at him. He waited. He could wait all day. She watched his boots. He shifted his weight and she heard a sharp brush against fabric. He held a pair of thick leather gloves within her view, lifted the hat brim and looked her in the eye.

"These are for you."

She took them and before she could form words he dropped the brim, turned and walked out of the study, across the dining room carpet, into the kitchen and out the back door. She slumped into her grandfather's chair and pulled the hat off her stinging ears.

"Thank you."

Later at supper, Jody's dining room chair sat glaringly empty. Buck shoveled his food the way he always did, and Whit ate quickly and left.

Livvy had stared at her plate during most of the meal. Anything other than catching Whit's eye and blushing with anger or humiliation. A fine line ran between those two emotions and tonight the delineation was even narrower.

"You ready to leave early?" Pop studied her over the coffee-filled teacup he held before his lips.

Livvy forced a smile. "Yes." She raised her head, assumed her role as fellow cowhand and cook. "I'll have biscuits, coffee and bacon ready for anyone who wants to eat before we leave."

Buck grinned at her and Pop grunted.

"I also have food for us at midday."

Her grandfather nodded and placed the delicate cup on its saucer. "We're not taking the wagon, you know."

"I have a sack of food, and if everyone has a canteen,

that will do." She laid her flatware across her plate and topped it with a linen napkin. "Do you have an extra one I could use?"

"Sure do. I'll bring it up from the barn along with mine to rinse out tonight." He looked at Buck. "You might want to do the same."

Buck nodded and wiped his mouth.

"Why don't you go to the barn and get 'em all right now?"

Buck glanced between Pop and the remaining sausages and potatoes on the serving platter, clearly struggling with his boss's request.

"Now."

"Yes, sir." Buck scooted from the table and lifted his plate. "I can take these to the kitchen if you'd like, Miss Livvy." He reached for the platter.

"Leave it."

At Pop's quick command, Buck snatched his hand back with a grimace.

"If there's any left when you get back with the canteens, you can have 'em."

Livvy prayed that Buck wouldn't toss her grandmother's china in the dishpan on his way out and sighed in relief as the back door opened and closed without a preliminary clatter of plate against metal. Her shoulders relaxed and the day's activity and drama seeped from her arms and left her empty and tired.

Pop reached for her hand. "You'll do fine tomorrow, Livvy. I know you will. You've got Baker blood in you."

She drank in his confidence and affection. "Thanks, Pop. I won't let you down."

"I'm not worried about that." He patted her fingers with his other leathered hand. "But I want you to be safe. That's why I want you to ride Ranger."

Shocked, Livvy met her grandfather's solemn gaze. "But he's your horse, Pop."

"That he is, but he's a good, sure-footed mount, and that's what you'll be needing out there in the rough." He released her hand, folded his arms on the table and leveled his steely eyes upon her.

"I know you and Whit sometimes have your squabbles. For a couple of preachers' kids you fight like two polecats. But he will show you exactly how things are done. Do what he tells you, watch for flying hooves, and you'll be fine."

Polecats?

Pop's eyes glistened and his mustache quirked. "Your grandmother would be proud."

Livvy banished the image of Whit as a polecat. "Did she ever work the roundup with you?"

A deep sigh threatened to cleave the dear man's chest. "Oh, yes. Our first year here, it was just the two of us roping and branding calves. Your mama helped, too, the little sprite. Had her on the stamp iron. We didn't have that many cows back then, but it was a sight to behold, this old cowboy and his two female hands."

He chuckled and light flickered in his gray eyes. Suddenly he slapped both hands on the table and pushed back. "Think I'll turn in. We've got a long day ahead with an early start."

Livvy stood and planted a kiss on his cheek. "If Buck doesn't hurry back I'll save these potatoes for tomorrow morning."

The back door banged open and Livvy flinched. Pop laughed.

"Got the canteens here for you, Miss Livvy."

She gathered the dishes and joined Buck in the kitchen. "Thank you. Set them on the counter there and find your fork. You can clean up the leftovers."

Buck grinned as if she'd given him an entire pie and

sat down at the work table to finish off the remains of their meal.

Livvy set the dishes in the pan, shaved in a soap curl and added hot kettle water. Three canteens lay on the counter.

"You brought only three canteens, Buck. Didn't you want to fill yours?"

He swallowed a mouthful. "Them's all there was. That one with the red stripe is mine. The other two must be your grandfather's and Whit's, unless Whit has one in his tack that I don't know about."

A tingling burn raced down Livvy's throat. How could she ask her grandfather to share his water? And she'd rather die of thirst than beg from Whit.

Tomorrow might be more difficult than she anticipated.

Chapter 10

A faint glow edged the distant rimrock. Whit itched to scale its face, find the cougar he knew lurked there, but other work needed tending to. He filled his lungs, drank in the scent of piñon, juniper and damp earth. A brief rain had cleared the air, settled the dust. Hidden birds twittered their predawn songs.

Oro snorted and tongued his bit, impatient to leave. Whit checked his cinch and stirrups, the oilcloth slicker he kept rolled behind his saddle, two ropes coiled and ready on the right side, a full canteen on the other.

He repeated the routine for a sleek bay mare and Baker's stout little gray gelding, Ranger. The man insisted that Livvy ride the gray. Whit shortened both stirrup straps a notch. Instead of a rope, the leather thong on her saddle snugged an old flour sack—Livvy's provisions for their midday meal. Her efforts dulled the irritation that chafed like a splinter under his chaps. But only slightly.

Buck should be checking his own mount, but he was probably still filling himself on Livvy's bacon and biscuits.

The kitchen door opened and pale yellow light spilled across the yard. Baker walked out followed by a slight-built boy. Had Jody Perkins wised up and returned in the night? His bunk had been empty this morning. Maybe he'd sneaked in before breakfast.

Anger churned in Whit's belly as he watched the pair move toward the hitching rail. Baker loosed the reins holding the sturdy bay and pulled himself into the saddle, stiff leg and all. The boy walked around to Ranger's left side, gathered the reins, and swung himself up with surprising grace. The move drew Whit's closer scrutiny. *Livvy.*

He should have recognized the hat.

Stifling a comment, he watched her set her booted feet in the stirrups. From his position on the ground, he could clearly see her eager eyes, her lips slightly parted as she settled in the seat, tested the stirrups. Her hair must be piled inside that toadstool she wore or else she'd whacked it off since last night.

She caught him with a shadowed look. "Just right. Thank you."

He jerked a nod and turned away.

"And for the gloves."

He stopped and spoke to his shoulder. "You're welcome."

He mounted Oro, waited for Buck to join them with the irons and then turned his back on the sunrise and headed toward the mountain. They'd ride to the top and work their way down. If everything went as he hoped, they'd be done in three days.

Dawn lit the top of Eight Mile Mountain and melted down the sides and into the grassland like warm butter. Whit led the small party halfway up the rough side of the mountain toward a park where he expected to find a good number of cow-calf pairs. He looked back to find Baker and Livvy holding their own. Buck brought up the rear.

An hour later at the edge of a long, low saddle, Whit rode through a thick timber stand and broke into a wide clearing. A flat park spread before them, eighty or ninety acres. More than fifty cows grazed with their calves beside them.

If he had enough men, he'd set up a bunch ground, build a fire and brand the calves up here. But it would take at least one other hand to hold the herd together while he roped and the others held them down and branded. He could tie 'em, but those little critters'd kick the bottom out of daylight, and if one of the mamas got on the hook, somebody would get hurt.

Baker insisted that Livvy brand, but Whit insisted she do it in a corral. He pulled up and whirled Oro to face his scraggly crew.

"Buck, you take the left. Mr. Baker, you go with him, and Livvy and I will take the right. We'll ease 'em out into the middle and drive 'em nice and slow through this break in the timber. Don't let them get in the trees. Any runaways on your side, Buck, you take 'em. I'll take any on mine. We'll push them all down into the upper corrals."

He looked at each person, waiting for agreement. Baker nodded and tugged his hat brim. Buck grinned and spun his horse around. Livvy swallowed and set her jaw.

Whit screwed his hat down and heeled Oro into an easy lope.

He skirted the park, drawing uplifted looks from a dozen cows that switched their tails and called their calves. Three maverick two-year-olds tossed their heads and broke from the herd. He hoped Buck would let them be. They didn't need a rodeo out here on the back of the mountain. He and Buck could always find those big fellas come fall, and if they didn't carry a brand, they'd build a fire and use the rings on them.

The wind in his face, Oro's strong rhythmic gait, the thrill of being part of something bigger—it all welled inside him. How could book learning ever replace this? He'd die if he had to work in a store or bank or anywhere but in this open country as a cowboy.

He looked back for Livvy. She was a length behind him, the gray keeping pace with Whit but no lust in its eye to race. Guess ol' Baker knew what he was doing putting his granddaughter on a horse that wasn't out to take the leader. He prayed she had as much horse sense as she claimed. Otherwise, they'd all be in for a Wyoming rodeo whether he wanted one or not.

He reined in next to Livvy and they slowed to a walk. "When we get behind them, we'll walk 'em toward that gap we just came through. You take the back and I'll ride ahead in case any try to break out through the trees."

Livvy met his gaze and nodded, her mouth clamped tight. No smile, no words, all business. But her eyes betrayed her excitement and burned like blue embers. How could he get her to look at him like that when riding wasn't involved?

He tightened his fingers on the reins and motioned for her to go on ahead. She touched her heels to the gray and loped ahead. She could ride, that was for certain. No daylight showed beneath her—well, no daylight showed where it shouldn't.

It just kept getting better.

Livvy tried not to lean into the wind, tried not to encourage Pop's cow pony to pick up speed, but she couldn't help it. Life surged through her veins with the beat of the gray's hooves, the scent of grass and pine and cattle—had she died and gone to heaven?

She longed to pull off her hat and let the wind whip through her hair. She laughed aloud and the sound fell away with visions of Whit Hutton set back on his heels, madder than a wet hen. She laughed again.

He resented her presence and she resented him for resenting her. How was that for a tune? She'd show him how much horsewoman she was. She'd show him that Pop's faith was not ill put.

The cattle began to bunch and move as a herd, away from her and toward the opening in the timber. She pulled up when she reached the end of the park, turned to face them, and leaned down to rub the gray's neck.

"You're a good one, Ranger. Good and even tempered and truehearted. Unlike a certain cowboy I could mention." She scanned the park for Whit and found him where he said he'd be—riding flank, slowly pushing the herd toward the break. To her right, Pop and Buck were doing the same. If they kept out of the trees, they might make the corrals by midday.

She glanced toward the sun, not yet straight overhead but hot as a skillet. She wiped her sleeve across her brow, grateful for the hat, regardless of Whit's mockery. She reached back to feel his gloves still tucked behind her waist. He wasn't all bad. Just bad enough to keep her guessing.

She'd never been so hot and cold over anyone in all her life. Well, not really hot and cold, more like hot and cool. Cold had never applied where Whit Hutton was concerned, and life would no doubt be easier if it had. He could set her blood to boiling with his arrogance and her heart to purring with his tenderness. What a maddening man.

Her eyes wandered to Pop riding easy on the big bay, his gray hat pulled low. He looked like any cowboy trailing a herd, not a man well up in years with a bad leg. What had he been like when he first met Mama Ruth? Had he been a striking cattleman who filled the young Englishwoman with spit and fire the way Whit did Livvy?

More laughter bubbled up from her insides like a mountain spring. What would her gentle mother say of such a phrase as *spit and fire?* Not at all ladylike, but altogether true. Her mother was proper, a real lady, but she could ride as well as any man and had been doing so long before Robert Hartman turned her head one Sunday morning in Cañon City. Sixteen, she'd been, but she'd known the man of her heart when she saw him. Why, Whit's father had married the two of them in an odd ceremony with three brides and three grooms.

With the deep pull of a strong current, Livvy realized that her connection to Whit—if she dared call it that—went back to before she was born.

A holler drew her attention. Buck leaned forward and slapped his coiled rope against his chaps, shouting at the cow that took to the timber. No wonder Whit had warned them all. In a moment Buck had vanished, swallowed by the thick woods, but whooping and hollering. *Lord, don't let him hit a tree or a low-hanging branch.*

Pop loped toward the leaders. Whit held his side and Livvy tightened her hands on the reins. A little bit farther and they'd be through to the other side and headed downslope toward the corrals.

The opening narrowed at the end, and Livvy heard Buck and the cow crashing through the underbrush. Several cows turned their heads toward the noise and suddenly the stray and her calf broke through the timber ahead of the herd with Buck hard on her tail. With a smooth, even motion he built a loop, swung it above his head and dropped it around the cow's horns. He turned his horse and dallied the rope around his saddle horn, jerking the cow around. The calf followed, its tongue hanging out from the hard run.

At an easy trot, Buck led the cow toward the open corral gate and in no time the others followed her through in a lowing stream of mottled brown and white and black. Pop and Whit rode through with them and Livvy shut the gate behind the milling cattle.

Buck ran his cow up against the fence, threw slack into his rope and popped the loop off her head. Then he opened another gate as Whit cut several calves from the herd. Buck and Pop steered them into the next pen and followed them through. Livvy rode around the outside. After twenty calves funneled into the second pen, Whit shut the middle gate.

Buck started a fire and laid in the irons. Livvy looped Ranger's reins around a corral pole, climbed to the top and waved her arms. Whit rode over.

"We can eat while the fire's building."

Whit looked at Buck and back to Livvy. He nodded curtly and dismounted, draping his reins on the top pole. Pop did the same and all three men squeezed between the poles to the outside.

Livvy took down her bag and set it on a rock a little ways from the corral. Using the sack as a tablecloth, she laid out the sliced bread and beef, a smaller bag of ginger cookies and what biscuits were left from breakfast. Pop leaned against the rock and Buck and Whit squatted nearby. Pop removed his hat, sleeved his brow and bowed his head.

"Thank You, Lord, for Your good help and this food. Amen."

Livvy smiled to herself. Pop had always been short on words, but he was long on heart. Certain that everyone else had enough to eat, she stacked bread and beef and made quick work of it, amazed at how hungry she was. She ate two cookies before remembering she had no water.

"Thank you, Livvy." Pop laid a hand on her shoulder and gave it a pat. "That hit the spot."

Buck raised his hat and grinned. "Thank you, ma'am. 'Specially for them cookies."

Whit stood and wiped his hands on his chaps. "You ready to get started?"

Ungrateful beast. "As soon as I clean up here." Livvy stashed the remainder and tied it on her saddle. She glanced around the clearing for a stream and found none. She'd have to wait.

All three men had returned to the corral and Whit was mounted, swinging his rope at a mottled calf.

She squeezed through the poles and pulled on the leather gloves. They fit perfectly, as if made for her. Had they been Whit's when he was younger and smaller? She grimaced at the thought. In order to follow her heart and be herself, she had to don the trappings of others—her grandmother's britches, Pop's hat and Whit's gloves.

The calf bawled when Whit's loop snagged its back legs and he dragged it to the fire. Her grandfather hop-skipped to the calf and pinned it to the ground with one knee, his stiff leg sticking out to the side.

Whit dallied and stepped off Oro, who stood stock-still, holding the rope taut on the calf. He grabbed an iron, returned to the calf and pressed the iron to its right hip. The hair sizzled and white smoke billowed around Whit, wrapping him in its cloud.

He stepped back and looked at Livvy. "That's how it's done. You up to it?"

She took the iron, walked to the fire and shoved it in the glowing coals. Whit mounted Oro, signaled him forward, and Pop loosed the slack rope and let the calf up. It bawled and raced to a corner with the others. Whit built another loop and dropped it beneath a second calf that stepped right in. The process repeated and Livvy prepared for the next victim.

No—not victim. She refused to see it that way. This

was their livelihood, the very food for their table and the tables of miners in mountain camps and people in Cañon City and elsewhere. This was life, and she chose to partake.

Buck handed her the hot iron. He should be holding the calves, not Pop, but she suspected her grandfather's pride had played into the arrangement. She glanced at Whit and found him watching her with squinted eyes. Taking a deep breath, she stepped to the calf, rotated the iron so the Bar-HB was upright and pressed it into the calf's right hip.

Instantly the hair singed and curled away to cinders. White smoke swirled up, enveloping her in the smell of scorched hide. She coughed from the acrid odor but pressed firmly with the iron.

"Good," Whit shouted.

She lifted the iron and stepped back.

"You don't need to cook 'em." A crooked grin flashed beneath his hat brim as he loosened his dally. Pop let the calf up.

Whit coiled his rope and built a loop for the next one. "Well, don't just stand there. Get the iron hot."

Livvy gritted her teeth. What had she expected? A pat on the back?

Her throat screamed for water and she looked at the other calves huddling in the corner. Were they as parched as she? At least she didn't have a stinging brand on her hip.

Chapter 11

Whit had to admit, Olivia Hartman could handle the branding just fine. He snarled, careful not to let her hear him. She'd be after his hide with that hot iron.

The next calf was a bull and Buck stepped in to hold a leg. Baker straddled the calf, pulled out his stock knife and with a quick grab and slice set the little fella's mind on other things. Whit glanced at Livvy, who stood watching, horrified. Obviously, she hadn't seen the cutting side of branding.

"Run and grab that cookie sack and bring it over. We'll have calf fries tonight," Whit said.

Livvy stood motionless, staring at him as if she were deaf.

"Go on, Livvy." Baker motioned toward her horse. "We can't hold him all day."

At her grandfather's word she squeezed through the pole corral and found the small sack. When she returned, Baker took it, dropped the tenders inside and snugged the mouth of the sack in his waist. By then Buck had the iron hot, and Livvy laid the Bar-HB against the bawling animal's hip.

She had grit, he'd give her that.

By day's end, they'd branded seventy calves and had enough fries for a feast tonight. Whit chose to let Baker explain to his granddaughter how to cook them.

While Buck kicked out the fire, Whit opened the inside gate and let the calves return to their mothers. Pop was back on his horse and rode through the herd to open the outside gate. With little encouragement, the lead cow saw her opportunity and dashed through. The others followed.

The taint of singed hair and hide hung in the air, and deep satisfaction coursed through Whit's veins. A good day. With what he and the Perkins brothers had accomplished earlier, they were more than a third of the way through the stock. If the cattle hadn't scattered too far, they might have this done in three days after all.

Whit brought up the rear on the ride home. From the way Baker and Livvy sat their horses, it looked as though they'd nearly worn themselves out. He worried more about Baker with his bum leg than Livvy. She'd held her own. But Baker's leg might not last. How could he get the man to take the fire and let Buck work the calves?

Livvy rode a few yards ahead and a sudden coughing fit drew her up. Whit leaned forward, setting Oro to a trot. He reined in beside her and looked for her canteen. She didn't have one.

He unlashed his own and held it out.

She scowled over the hand across her mouth.

Had she gone loco? "Here, take a drink." He pushed the canteen toward her chest. With a final stabbing glare, she took it, removed the top and drank like a drunkard.

"Did you really think you could go all day and breathe all that smoke and not need water?"

She coughed again and wiped her mouth on her sleeve, avoiding his eyes. "I don't have a canteen."

Infuriating woman. "Why didn't you say something?"

She stared straight ahead.

"You can have that one."

She held it out to him. "Thank you, but no, thank you."

He kicked his horse too hard and Oro lunged ahead in a hard trot, then settled to an easy lope. He passed Baker and a few choice words from his boss's colorful vocabulary jumped into Whit's mind as he rode by.

Rather than voice his frustration at female wrangling, he pulled up next to Buck, whose horse marched against a tight rein. "I'm glad you didn't try to chase down those two mavericks up there today. We can get 'em later."

Buck's mount had the home pastures in his nose and was in a hurry to get there. "I figured as much." He checked the reins and the horse slowed. They rode a ways in silence before Buck shared his thoughts.

"She did all right, didn't she?"

Whit slid a sideways glance at the boy. "Yeah, she did all right. But she nearly choked to death on the smoke."

Buck scrubbed his hand over his face.

"What?" Whit knew that nervous gesture.

"We didn't have enough. When Baker had me bring 'em in last night, I could only find three canteens. Why didn't she say something to the boss?"

"Why does a woman do anything she does?"

Buck guffawed and Whit threw him a warning glare. "She can have mine. I've got one in the bunkhouse."

"I figured Baker'd have a couple extra."

"Did you ask him?"

Buck rubbed his face again. "No, sir. Didn't see him after supper and I didn't think about it this morning."

"She's got one now."

Whit heeled Oro ahead and they loped down the final

slope onto the bottom pasture. The sun slanted low across the valley and washed the house and barns in a long yellow light. Gray clouds bunched above the rimrock beyond, and a distant rumble echoed off the mountains to the north. There'd come a rain tonight.

Crossing Wilson Creek, Whit noted it ran wider than two days ago, swollen with summer storms. He hoped they didn't get more than a light rain tonight. They didn't need a flood spreading out and running in close to the buildings. He looked again at the bunching clouds and flinched at another thunder roll, louder this time, closer.

A fickle woman, the weather.

Whit felt the sneer on his lips as he rode into the yard and pulled up by the barn. *Fickle* didn't begin to describe Livvy. She was up to her old tricks again—fire and ice.

He brushed Oro and turned him loose in the near pasture to roll and shake and feed on sweet creek-watered grass. Buck rode in next, followed by Baker and Livvy. Whit headed for the bunkhouse. If he wasn't half-starved he'd skip supper. But the bulge in the bottom of the cookie bag made his mouth water. He hoped Livvy got it right.

To his great relief, she did.

She must have left beans in the stove all day, because the pork-laced aroma wrapped around him when he stepped through the back door. Above it lay the crispy lure of calf fries sizzling on the stovetop. Livvy wore an apron over her denims and her loose hair fell down her back like a wild horse mane.

He'd marry that woman if she'd give him half a chance.

Disgusted, he stomped back out. He must be as barn-soured as Buck's horse, having such thoughts. He scrubbed his hands and arms for the second time and splashed cold water on his face and head. He combed his fingers through his hair, dried his hands and met Buck at the door on his way in.

"You'd better wash up if you don't want a tongue lashin'."

Buck grinned. Whit swore it was the only reaction the boy had, regardless of the situation.

Livvy laid the work table in the kitchen for supper, too tired for the usual formal setting in the dining room. She doubted Pop would mind. After he'd told her how to cook the calf fries, he had retired to his room. She'd heard his boots thump to the floor as he pulled them off and the bed squeak when he lay down.

Poor man. If he were half as sore and worn as she, he'd be needing his liniment tonight. She checked the corner cabinet to make sure they had enough. She might even borrow a little herself.

Grudgingly she admitted that what she was frying in the big skillet smelled enticingly good, if only she could banish the knowledge of their origin. When Buck and Whit finally showed up, Buck wore his usual mindless grin and Whit looked about ready to drool.

Men. It didn't take much to please them when they were tired and hungry.

Her heart turned at the thought, and sadness knifed beneath her ribs. How pleasant it would have been to ride beside Whit today if he hadn't been so certain she couldn't do her part with the branding. Well, she had shown him.

And what had he shown her?

Kindness. The knife pressed deeper. He'd noticed her coughing fit and offered to share his water. Insisted, in fact. She scooped more beans onto his plate and topped them with several fries.

She set a plate before him as well as Buck and Pop. Buck's eyes darted between his helping and Whit's, and a rare frown wrinkled his usually smooth brow. Heat rushed up Livvy's neck at the obvious favoritism she'd shown, and leaving her own plate on the table, she quickly turned away.

"You men go ahead. I'll get Pop. He went to rest for a moment."

"I think she likes you better." Buck's hoarse whisper followed Livvy as she hurried through the dining room. The flush climbed into her cheeks. At least Whit couldn't see her.

Pop's muffled snore met her at the doorway to his room and she regretted having to wake him. But if he rode again tomorrow, he'd need every morsel of food for strength. She'd make sure he had several eggs for breakfast.

She touched his shoulder. "Pop?"

He groaned.

Fear took a lick at her heart. "Are you all right?"

"I'll be fine. Give me a minute to get my bearings." He sat up and swung his legs over the edge of the bed, flinching with the effort.

"Would you rather eat in here?"

He waved her off with an impatient hand. "No, girl, I'm not dyin', I'm just stove-up." He pushed himself up and softened his tone with a wink. "After supper you can find that liniment your grandmother always kept on hand. It will do me some good tonight."

Livvy slipped an arm around his waist on pretense of affection, but as she hoped, he laid an arm across her shoulder and they walked together. By the time they reached the kitchen, he had straightened and entered under his own power.

Did men ever grow old enough to not strut and preen?

Pop slid a chair out and dropped into it with a grunt. "Whit, you say the blessing tonight."

Buck's spoon stopped halfway to his mouth and Whit coughed on a biscuit. Livvy tucked her chin to hide her surprise and seated herself next to her grandfather.

Whit cleared his throat and glanced up as he bowed his head, catching Livvy's eye before closing his.

"Thank You, Lord, for Your help today, for keeping us all safe. And thank You for this bounty and the company we have in one another. Amen."

Did Whit count her as one of the company for which he was thankful?

Pop bit into a fry and followed it with beans. "Fine job, Livvy. Fine job. Aren't you going to try your own cooking?"

She kept her head down, stirring her beans. "Maybe later." She couldn't look these men in the eye, knowing what they ate and relished as they did so.

Whit chuckled. Buck shoveled. Livvy prayed for someone to change the subject.

Pop obliged. "Buck, my leg is stiff as a stamp iron. Why don't you let me take over the fire tomorrow and you flank calves?"

Livvy bit the inside of her mouth to keep from thanking God out loud. She dared not insult the man's pride—or good judgment. She sighed and relaxed shoulders she hadn't realized were tight. Thank God, indeed.

Whit nodded as he chewed and looked Pop in the eye. "Good call, sir." He traded his spoon for his coffee cup and took a swallow. "I'm thinkin' most of the cattle are up the northeast draw, over in the far park. That pole corral up there might hold forty, fifty head at a time, but we could drive 'em all down, let 'em graze and rotate 'em in."

No one commented. Too tired, Livvy supposed, and she wasn't about to say anything. She had borne enough of Whit's scowling looks through the day. Instead she savored the beans and biscuits and lamented the fact that she could not fall immediately into bed. Not with preparations for tomorrow's meal awaiting her after the men left.

"I agree." Pop wiped his mouth, downed his coffee and

pushed back from the table. "Get me that liniment, Livvy, and I'm gonna turn in."

She retrieved it from the cupboard and picked up a small piece of toweling. "I can help you, Pop."

"No." The curt hand wave stopped her. "You have enough to do tonight. We'll be leavin' at the same time and needin' the same food as you brought today." He took the towel and bottle. "See you all then."

At the dining room door, he paused and turned his head to the side. "Good job today. That includes you, Livvy."

Full of glory at her grandfather's remark, she stood by the stove and watched him hobble through the dining room. At the fireplace he stopped, opened the gaudy French clock on the mantel and wound it, turning the key four times. She counted, the way she did every night when he tended Mama Ruth's favored timepiece.

Returning to the table, she caught Whit's dark eyes above the cup he held to his lips. He watched her take her seat, pick up her spoon and swallow the rest of her beans whole. Why did he have to stare?

"I agree," he said, parroting Pop's earlier words.

She met his look head on, her nerves steeled by her grandfather's confidence. "About what?"

"Today." Both elbows rested on the table, the cup held aloft in his rough hands. "You did a good job."

The compliment shot heat beneath her already too-warm skin. She lowered her gaze and lifted a napkin to her mouth. "Thank you."

"Got any more beans?"

God bless Buck Perkins. In his typically awkward manner, he delivered her from what could have been an awkward moment.

"Of course." She took his bowl to the stove and ladled in an extralarge helping. She had no doubt in the boy's ability to finish it off.

Suddenly fatigued, she bent beneath the ache in her back and legs and moaned inwardly at the thought of rising an hour earlier than they planned to leave so she could make biscuits and eggs and bacon.

Whit stood, gathered his bowl, and took it to the dishpan. "Thank you." His gaze traveled the swath of hair that had fallen over her shoulder. "See you in the morning."

He grabbed his hat on his way out and looked at Buck. "Hurry up. We leave at daybreak."

Buck shoveled, scooted his chair and sleeved his mouth nearly all at once. Livvy shook her head at the boy's ability to be so effortlessly mannerless.

"Thank you, ma'am." He handed her his dishes. "Mighty good."

She gave him a weary smile. "See you tomorrow morning."

Chapter 12

On the third morning, the clock in Whit's head woke him to the tuneless racket of Buck snoring. *Snorting* was more like it. The kid gagged like a choked bull.

The roundup's second day had gone much like the first, and Whit hoped today would be their last. In fact, he did more than hope, he prayed. He'd smelled rain on the breeze the last two nights and didn't want to get caught in a storm today.

He pulled on his pants and boots, knotted his bandanna and tucked in his shirt. He kicked Perkins's bunk on his way outside. "Get up. Daylight's burnin'."

Wasn't burning, wasn't even smoldering, but by the time the kid made it to the kitchen it would be. They had farther to ride today and needed a fast start.

He gathered three horses, checked their hooves, saddled them, and led them to the hitching rail behind the house. The square light of the kitchen window pulled at his belly and his heart as he watched Livvy at the stove doing what she did best. One of many things, he grudgingly admitted. She was definitely full of skill and surprises. Maybe he'd get a few moments alone with her before Baker and Buck showed up.

But he'd not be apologizing for his earlier behavior. He was justified in his concern for his men, for the cattle. For her. They were his responsibility. Hauling a woman in to do a man's job was not. Lucky for her it had turned out all right.

Lucky for him.

He pulled his hat off, stepped through the back door and into the warm, yellow light.

She looked up from the stove, a pleased expression tilting her mouth in a pink curve. "Good morning."

"Mornin'." So far, so good. He straddled a chair.

"Coffee?" She brought the pot and two mugs to the table, set one before him and filled it with the dark, steamy liquid.

He nodded his thanks and took the cup in both hands, pulled the hot brew through his lips. "Hmm."

She poured another cup and sat down.

He glanced at the stove.

"Don't worry. Breakfast is ready. I'm waiting for everyone to show up so we can all eat at once rather than in shifts."

She had pulled her long hair back into a single plait. He felt a twinge of disappointment. "Your grandfather not up?"

She sipped. "He's up, but moving slow."

A faint trace of liniment mingled with the coffee's strong aroma. He leaned toward her and sniffed. "Did you rub him down?"

She blushed like the sky at dawn and hid behind her mug. Two laughing eyes peered over the top. "I was a little sore myself after two days, so when he fell asleep last night, I stole in and borrowed the bottle."

He chuckled at her admission. Another surprise. "I guess you might be. How long has it been since you rode?"

"It's been awhile. There was no riding on our last visit for Mama Ruth's funeral."

The memory stripped the smile from her eyes and replaced it with sorrow. He longed to bring the light back, tip her mouth in that pink curve.

Baker walked in with a more pronounced limp as Buck came through the back door. Whit looked at his crew gathering around the table and prayed again. This time for a miracle. They'd need it if they were going to get the rest of the calves branded today and not get someone busted up.

Pop gave thanks and Livvy served bacon, biscuits with white gravy, and eggs, and kept everyone's coffee hot and full. She ate standing at the counter as she packed her larder bag and filled the canteen Whit had given her. Good thing he saw her—he'd forgotten to fill his.

"I'll be right back and then we'll leave." He took his dishes to the sink, gave Livvy what he hoped she'd consider a friendly smile and beat it out the back door.

By the time he returned to the house, everyone was mounted. He filled the canteen at the outside pump and draped it over his saddle horn.

Oro rumbled deep in his chest and pawed the ground. "Enough." Whit slapped him good-naturedly on the neck, slipped the reins from the rail and swung into the saddle. Buck carried the irons, Livvy had her bag and everyone had a canteen. He turned Oro toward the east.

Dawn peeked above the rimrock, flattened by a dark blanket that glowed orange and pink at the edges. Not a good sign. Whit drew in a deep breath and with it the promise of a storm.

They rode toward the jagged rock wall and Whit

scanned its shadowed lip. Near the base they turned north to follow the draw around a low hill. A scream split the air.

Another scream behind him, and he whirled to see Livvy with Ranger's reins pulled to her chest. The horse danced backward, bouncing its front feet off the ground.

"Let up!" He charged toward her and pulled up next to the rearing gray. "Let up on the reins!" Leaning out, he jerked her hands toward the saddle horn.

As soon as the reins went slack, Ranger stopped. He stood trembling and his eyes rolled white at the fear he'd picked up from his rider.

Breathless and pale, Livvy held Whit with frightened eyes, her fingers clutching the reins with an iron grip. Whit's doubts returned and dug in their spurs.

"Easy. Easy." He spoke low, as much to Livvy as to the horse.

Pop loped over and grabbed the gray by its headstall. "He'll flip over backward if you yank on him like that."

"I—I know. It just startled me." Livvy's chest heaved on every word and her hands shook.

She released one hand and leaned down to pat Ranger's neck. She looked to Whit. "What was that?"

Whit laid his hand atop hers on the horn, gave it a light squeeze. "A lion. Up on the rimrock. But it's all right— she won't come down here."

"Why does she scream like that? Did she kill something?"

Whit withdrew his hand, looked at Pop, who let go of Ranger, and moved away. "She's lonely."

A bit more than lonely, more like calling for a mate, but Whit wasn't about to go into that. Livvy ducked her head. She'd figured it out.

Buck had ridden back at the commotion. "It's enough to chill your blood for sure."

Livvy raised her chin and heeled Ranger ahead. "She caught me off guard, that's all."

And that was exactly how Whit felt—caught off guard by a beautiful woman out in the breaks where she didn't belong, nearly getting crushed beneath her horse. He had never believed in omens, not with his God-fearing folks. But the stormy dawn and bloodcurdling cat cry didn't bode well for the day ahead. He tugged his hat down and loped back to the front of their small string. If any other surprises awaited them, he wanted to take the brunt.

Livvy's insides quaked and she concentrated on appearing calm and in control of her emotions. She might be able to fool the men but not Ranger. His neck arched and his ears pricked and his walk was more of a nervous trot. Truth be told, she wanted to wheel him and run him as fast as he could go back to the ranch house and hide beneath the quilts on her bed.

Lord, help her! The fright in Whit's eyes tore into her nearly as deep as the cat's scream. Was he afraid *for* her or *because* of her?

The red horizon faded to pink and into a blinding white as the sun climbed above low clouds. Daylight spread slowly over the hills and dripped into the ravines and creek beds. Blackbirds and robins called to one another across the meadows and hawks screed above them. How could such beauty hide such chilling terror?

By midday they had driven the cattle down to a new pole corral and had half the cow-calf pairs inside. Whit refused to eat until they had finished branding every single calf. Argument danced on the tip of Livvy's tongue, begging to spring to life, but she bit it back and followed his orders. It helped to believe his sharp commands were directed to his branding crew and not to her personally.

Only twice did she stop for water, and she noticed with

satisfaction that the men took a break at the same time. Against Whit's wishes, she passed out two cookies to each man and quickly downed one herself. She worried more about Pop's strength than her own, and if Whit gave her any grief, that was exactly what she'd tell him.

The sun balanced on the western peaks by the time they loosed the last calf. Livvy pulled her gloves and hat off and sleeved her brow as she watched the youngsters run to their mamas seeking comfort for their burned hides. She almost felt guilty. But cattle from several different spreads roamed the mountains and parks together, and ranchers had to keep them straight.

Before each calf was branded, Whit read the markings on the cow. If it didn't carry the Bar-HB, he'd holler out the brand and Buck would heat the rings. Livvy didn't know how to use the hot brass cinch rings, so Buck burned in a neighbor's brand that matched the one on the calf's mama.

But most of the little ones were her grandfather's. The recent bunch huddled with the cows at the west end of the corral. Something about their lowing gave her pause, and she considered the way they pressed hard against the far poles.

As Buck stomped out the fire, she walked to the railing and looked at the pairs outside, all bunching together facing the west with their rumps to the east. She looked over her shoulder and saw black-bellied clouds spilling off the northern mountains. A deep rumble rolled around them and a fat raindrop hit her arm.

The cattle knew.

Her grandfather opened the far gate and let the corralled pairs out. They ran to join the others pressing toward the far end of the park, away from the storm. Livvy shoved her hat on, tucked her gloves in her waist and ran to the gray. Buck and Whit were already mounted and she joined them.

"Should we ride into the trees?"

Whit and Pop both shook their heads.

"No," Pop said.

"But we'd be out of the rain, a little more protected." It seemed the only logical thing to do.

"And asking to be fried." Whit pushed his hat down and turned toward the draw they had come through earlier. "It's comin' a storm, and we don't want to be in the trees when the lightning hits. We'll find a bunch of low rocks and hunker down on the south side."

With that he kicked Oro into a lope and the others followed. Livvy had no choice but to do the same.

A sharp riflelike crack tossed Ranger's head nearly into Livvy's face. A fiery bolt fingered from the clouds and into the ground, and thunder bounced off far canyon walls and rolled across the park. Whit spurred Oro toward a red sandstone outcropping.

They managed to get off their horses before the downpour hit. Livvy gripped the gray's reins and pressed herself against the sandstone.

"Let him go." Pop jerked his head toward Ranger. "If he spooks, he'll run home."

Livvy noticed that the men weren't holding their horses. Reluctantly, she tossed the leather straps over Ranger's neck. The horse trotted off, swiveling his ears.

Another crack and Livvy flinched. She slid down, pulled her knees to her chest, and tried to squeeze her entire body beneath her hat brim. Rain pounded her back and bounced off the ground. *Bounced?* She looked closer and saw white kernel-size hail popping out of the grass. It stung her back and arms but there was nothing she could do.

Whit ran to his horse and unlashed a yellow roll behind his saddle. Then he joined Livvy, shook out the roll and with the slicker spread above him like wings, he squatted next to her, covering her with the yellow shield. Grateful for his body warmth, she pressed close to him as hail

pelted against the oilcloth. She laid her head on her knees
and looked at the man who huddled closer than was proper.
He grinned—that boylike smirk that could fan an angry
fire or stir a deep longing.

Oh, Lord, help her.

As they waited out the storm, Whit's arm lowered until
it rested on her shoulders. Even through her wet shirt his
heat seeped into her. Rivulets formed around their feet and
cut paths through the grass. Lightning hit close enough to
strike with the thunder, leaving no gap between. She expected the horses to bolt and run. They'd all be walking
back to the ranch after the storm. In the dark.

Thoughts of the mountain lion shivered through her,
adding to the chill of her wet clothes. Whit pulled her
closer and she didn't resist. She took off her soaked hat and
his breath warmed her. She lost herself in his dark eyes
while hail drummed in her ears. Or was that her heartbeat?

He didn't have to lean far. His lips brushed her hair and
a raspy moan escaped them.

It was definitely the hail that pounded in Livvy's temples, for her heart had surely stopped. If she dared raise
her face to him, she'd kiss him back. Right here beneath
his slicker with Buck and her grandfather hunkered down
Lord knew how close. Then Whit would think she was a
lightskirt.

Oh, Lord—again—help!

As if in immediate answer, the rain stopped. Suddenly
and completely. Livvy sucked in a breath and held it, listening. Whit raised his right arm and looked out. It was
over. He stood and shook out the slicker.

Livvy's legs screamed as she straightened, but she
clamped her mouth tight. No complaining, especially not
when her grandfather must have suffered terribly, hunkered down in the rain. She spun in a circle. Where was he?

He hobbled out between two rocks, his hat a wet, floppy

mess. Buck looked as bad but without the limp, and he trotted off to gather the horses that had wandered to a shimmering aspen grove. So much for being struck by lightning in the trees.

No birds sang, no cattle lowed, only the drip, drip, dripping of rain-drenched trees. The storm snagged on the western peaks and the sun slipped from view.

They had little time to ride home before full dark.

Chapter 13

Whit's chest thundered and it had not one thing to do with lightning and hail.

She hadn't pulled away. Nor had she slapped him. But how would he look her in the eye now that she knew she'd tangled his spurs?

Livvy smelled sweeter than new grass on a spring morning. Even under that oilcloth after a full day's work.

He was in deep trouble.

Buck brought the horses round. Whit checked his cinch and retied his slicker. The sun tucked tail and ran, and there'd be no moon with the cloud cover. If they didn't want to let their horses lead them, they'd best be going.

Baker looked as though he'd been rode hard. In fact, he had. They all had, and on empty stomachs. Good thing he hadn't given in to Livvy's talk about keeping their strength up. They could have been caught in the corral with a bunch of spooked cattle and had to come back tomorrow and chase 'em all down again.

As it was, his tally showed they'd branded most all the new calves. Course there'd always be more through the year, what with the bulls running loose. But he'd keep everyone close tomorrow, stay to home. The few head they might have missed could wait until Jody got back.

If he got back.

But Baker, at least, needed the rest. If the old man took sick and died, Whit would blame himself the rest of his days.

Buck rode up, wet as a duck.

"You still have both irons and the rings?" Whit said.

The boy nodded and slapped his saddle. "Right here where I tied 'em."

Baker walked his bay in closer and his hat flopped over his eyes. He lifted it with a finger and revealed a dripping mustache. "What are we waitin' on?"

Whit choked down a chuckle and reined Oro around. Thanks to his slicker, Livvy had fared better than her grandfather and Buck. He couldn't keep his mouth from lifting with pleasure at the memory of her tucked beneath his arm—and her soft yellow hair against his lips. He pulled his hat down, hoping to block her scrutiny. No sense in having her think he was laughing at her.

But it wasn't laughter that hitched his heart for Olivia Hartman. It was anything but. He spurred Oro into a lope and headed through the draw on the last thread of light.

By the time they reached the ranch house, the clouds had scattered and stars washed the sky to nearly daylight. Whit reined in, prompting Baker and Livvy to do the same. "Buck and I will take the horses."

Baker angled a resentful glare his way, but stepped down and handed Whit the reins.

"I can unsaddle my own horse." Livvy bowed up the way she always did when her independence was threatened.

"I know you can." Whit scowled, put gravel in his voice. "But I don't cook so good and I figure everyone is hungry."

"Well, if you had let us stop and—"

The scowl must have stopped her, for she caught her words in her teeth and clamped her mouth shut. She stepped off, untied the soaked larder sack and went to the house.

About time she did something his way without an argument.

Wet leather. Wet saddle blankets. Wet clothes. Whit nursed memories of the Saturday-night baths he'd grumbled over at his parents' house. What he wouldn't give to soak in a tub of hot water tonight.

He and Buck laid out the tack, turned the horses into the near pasture and slopped through mud to the bunkhouse to change clothes before supper. After that downpour, at least their bodies were clean.

When they stepped into the kitchen, the smells of fried potatoes and bacon and beans hit Whit in the gut. Livvy wore her blue dress and apron but stood at the stove in her stocking feet. She caught the question on his face and grinned like Buck.

"Pop built a fire and we put our boots on the hearth. Why don't you two do the same? Socks, too, if you don't mind eating barefoot."

Whit wasn't so sure he wanted to smell Buck's wool socks warming up while he ate. But dry boots sounded too good to turn down.

Baker sat in an overstuffed chair by the dining room fireplace, his stocking feet crossed before him on the fancy carpet. Buck dropped to the floor and started yanking on his boots. Whit returned to the back door, where he knew a bootjack waited. Two smooth pulls, and he carried his sodden boots to the hearth. He'd grease them tomorrow, help keep them drier the next time he got caught in the rain.

"Supper's on." Livvy set the beans on the dining table and returned to the kitchen. Whit noticed the fancy china plates already there, cups and spoons and knives in place. He shook his head. Didn't take her long to get them all feeling at home.

She returned with the coffee. "Well, are you going to eat or sit by the fire?" She poured each cup full and set the pot on a thick cloth.

Baker grunted as he shoved out of his chair and moved to the head of the table like an old bull favoring a new injury. Buck was a two-year-old coming into his own, rangy and full of himself. Livvy shone like a yellow filly with her hair hanging down her back, still damp from the rain. Whit—he just wanted to wrap his hands in that mane and hold on tight.

He coughed to clear his throat and head and took his place to Baker's right. Baker caught his eye and gave him a quick nod that Whit interpreted as an order to say grace. Guess it naturally fell to him as a preacher's son. Baker was calling on him to do so more often.

"Oh, Lord, You are mighty good to us. Thank You again for keeping us all safe in the storm. Give us strength from this good meal. Amen."

"Amen" echoed round the table, and Livvy served heaping helpings of beans and bacon and biscuits. Happiness hovered over her like a plum tree in full bloom, and she had a smile for each man as she set his plate before him. She served Whit last and her cheeks pinked as she glanced at him.

"Thank you." Whit shoved his longing down to his damp socks and turned his attention to the full plate.

"We goin' back tomorrow?" Buck tossed the question out between two bites.

"No." Whit took control before Baker could intervene. "My tally book says we're near done with only a handful left to check. We can finish when Jody gets back. I figure we all need to rest tomorrow, and there's plenty to do around here. Fences to mend. Hay needs cuttin'."

He slid a look at Baker, who worked on his food and kept his eyes down but not his voice.

"Buck, you mend the garden fence with that roll of wire I brought back and start on the hay. Whit can soap tack, fix what needs fixin' in the near pasture, and check on the widow Overton." Pop lifted his gaze to Livvy. "You need anything in town?"

She laid her spoon aside and dabbed her perfectly clean mouth with a napkin, but Baker spoke before she had a chance.

"Take the wagon in tomorrow and get what you need."

"We are nearly out of coffee and a few other things. And I'll get another bottle of liniment from Doc Mason."

"You know I have an account at Whitaker's."

She gave her grandfather a loving look that almost made Whit jealous.

"I can get the mail, too." She picked up her coffee and held it before her as if debating a proposition. "If I leave enough food prepared, do you think you could get by without me for a day?"

Whit's heart jumped into his throat, ready to bust out of his mouth in a loud "no!"

Baker leaned back against his chair and considered Livvy's request a moment. "And what takes a whole day in town?"

She placed her cup in its saucer and dropped her hands to her lap. "I want to stop and see Martha Hutton." Her face flushed a bit but she pressed on, keeping her eyes off Whit and fixed on her grandfather.

"When Whit and I were in town last, Mrs. Hutton said I could stop by any time. I'd like to take her up on that. For a visit."

Whit would go with her.

Baker smiled for the first time in several days. "I think that is a fine idea, Livvy. You need other women's company. Stay the night. I'd rather you not drive back alone near dark, and the three of us can hold this place together in the meantime."

But if Whit went with her... *The three of us?*

Her smile ravished the fire's light and kindled anxiety in Whit's mind. Livvy gone? For an entire day and night?

Gratitude flooded Livvy's heart for her grandfather's generous understanding, but her mind raced at the sudden shock plastered across Whit's face. He'd blanched white as her apron and looked as if he'd swallowed a boiled egg whole.

She felt his eyes following her as she refilled coffee cups and cleared her dishes to the kitchen. She had to get away from his scrutiny. She had to *breathe*. The tension between them was stifling and she prayed that her grandfather and Buck didn't pick up on it. Of course, Buck didn't pick up anything that didn't go into his mouth, so she was safe there.

But Pop was not easily duped. Not that she was sneaking around or doing anything she shouldn't. Warmth flooded her neck at the memory of riding out the storm beneath Whit's slicker.

Too much heat, that's what it was. She opened the back window and let the night air rush in, cool and fresh after the storm. A hesitant moon edged above the rimrock, and she shuddered, remembering the lion lurking there. *Lonely,* Whit had said. That meant only one thing in the animal world. Her neck flamed again. Goodness—could she not think of anything without flaring like a wind-driven wildfire?

As much as she longed to fall across her bed, she needed

work to keep her mind on more suitable thoughts. And she had plenty of it before leaving tomorrow. Another roast in the oven, fresh bread. She'd sweeten the deal by leaving Annie Hutton's apple butter on the kitchen table for the men to enjoy in her absence. A small price to pay for a day in town and a chance to visit with other women. *Whit's* women. *Oh, dear.*

She busied herself as the men filed out and off to bed, and she finally settled into the mundane chores of washing dishes and preparing food that required little if any conscious thought. An entire day with Annie and Marti Hutton held as much anticipation for her now as Christmas morning had as a child.

With the Dutch oven banked at the back of the stove, and the fireplace cooling in the dining room, Livvy dragged herself to bed, too tired to pack but mentally going over what to gather in the morning. Her back and legs ached from the less-than-customary movements required in branding. She longed to soak in a hot bath, one of the luxuries of her parents' Denver parsonage.

Pop had a fancy copper tub—Mama Ruth had insisted years ago. But Livvy was too tired to drag it out and wait for enough water to boil for even a warm bath, much less a hot one. Her pitcher and basin would have to meet her needs tomorrow.

In the morning Livvy startled awake, only mildly surprised to see that she'd fallen asleep across her bed still wearing her house dress and apron. The mantel clock struck five. Daylight teased at her window and birds warbled out a welcome. She hurried to the kitchen to check the roast, set water to boiling and put the bread in the oven.

After her morning bathing ritual, she chose a fresh dress and buttoned on her Sunday shoes. She spent longer on her hair, coiling it tightly at the base of her neck, and laid out her best bonnet.

The aroma of baking bread drew her back to the kitchen to thump the brown loaves with a finger. Perfect. She smiled, pleased with her culinary skills and aching only slightly from her recently acquired wrangling talents.

In her excitement she'd forgotten to gather eggs. She hurried to her room to change shoes and rushed outside with the basket on her arm. Thank goodness Buck would be mending the garden fence. Deer had ravaged her radishes and kale—even nibbled the rhubarb. At least they'd left the herbs and lavender alone.

Did they eat columbines, those lovely purple flowers she'd first seen during the picnic lunch she'd packed for the crew? Her pulse quickened at the memory and she forced her thoughts to the hens.

She gathered a dozen eggs to feed the men this morning and left three beneath a brooding hen. She must mention the cross old thing at breakfast so whoever gathered eggs would let her be.

Ha! As if the men cared to gather eggs in her absence.

She rinsed the eggs beneath the kitchen pump and set them on a towel. The coffee began to boil and she moved the pot a bit and spooned bacon grease into the big skillet. Fresh bread and eggs and coffee should fill everyone. With a sudden flurry, she whisked the apple butter off the table and hid it behind the egg basket. Let them find it after she left rather than finish it off this morning.

At the sound of her grandfather shuffling through the dining room, she cracked the first eggs into the skillet.

"Smells mighty good in here." His mustache hitched in a smile as he came to the stove and reached for the coffee. "Like it did when your grandmother started the day with her fine cooking."

Again, Livvy's heart swelled at his compliment. She had come all this way to help, and she took pride in knowing she had succeeded. Surely that kind of pride was not a sin. Even the woman in Proverbs 31 knew that her work was good.

Pop tucked a couple of coins in her apron pocket. "Give those to Doc Mason for Tad's care. And if he's able, bring the boy back with you and we'll get him home."

"That's very generous of you, Pop, but are you sure you will be all right today and this evening without me?"

His gray eyes twinkled as he sipped from a stoneware mug. "I will do just fine. But I won't hazard a guess where Whit is concerned. I daresay he might pine away while you're gone."

Livvy's sudden gasp brought a chuckle, and he made his way to the kitchen table, where he eased into a chair and extended his leg.

She turned to the eggs popping in the too-hot grease and pulled the skillet away.

"Don't be so surprised, Livvy, girl. That boy is already roped and snubbed. No other reason explains him spreading his slicker over you in a storm fit to drown a goose when he could have kept it for himself."

He knew. That meant Buck did, too. Oh, Lord, help her. Heat leaped from the stove to her face, she was certain. If only she were not so fair skinned, she could ward off the blush. Maybe if she didn't wear the bonnet, let the sun burn her face on the way to town, she'd have an excuse for her constantly flaming cheeks.

"You could do worse, Livvy."

She stole a peek at her grandfather's face. He watched her with a keen eye, as if measuring her reaction to his words. "He reminds me of myself when I was young and wanting my own spread. He's a good man—with the upbringing he's had, better than I was. You would do well to give him a chance."

Livvy flipped three eggs and broke the yolk in every one. She could not discuss such things with her grandfather, even though she knew the man loved her dearly. She set the ruined eggs on a plate for herself and broke three more into the skillet. She must get them right or she'd not have enough to feed the men.

Dare she tell Pop that his foreman had already turned her heart as well as her head?

Buck blustered through the backdoor, his perpetual grin beating him into the room. "Bess is all hitched and ready to go, Miss Livvy. The buckboard's out back here ready whenever you are."

Whit followed, apparently not nearly as pleased with Buck's news. He tossed his hat on a chair and took a seat with as surly an attitude as Livvy had yet seen.

She bit the inside of her mouth to squelch a laugh. He looked the way he had as a boy when his ma made him sit out of a game. Well, she'd cut him some slack this morning, not laugh in his face. She wanted him to treat her with grown-up grace. The least she could do was return the favor.

As Livvy expected, the men ate heartily and quietly, apparently enjoying the fruit of her labors. Deeply satisfied, she almost regretted leaving them to their own devices. Almost. A day and night with two bright, intelligent women outshone even the lilacs that bloomed round the ranch house.

And they would be here when she returned—the lilacs. And Whit.

Chapter 14

If Buck didn't swallow that stupid grin, Whit would feed it to him fist first and tamp it down with a stamp iron.

Fine thoughts for a preacher's son.

He swigged the hot coffee, hoping to burn away the fact that Livvy was riding into town alone and was as happy about it as a sparrow at a wormhole.

Baker was in a chipper mood, as well, which made it all worse somehow. Soaping tack was not the work Whit needed today. He needed bronc busting, maverick chasing, hard riding—something to wear him out and down to nothing.

He needed to drive Livvy to town himself.

And he'd have better luck skinning a live skunk than getting that idea past Baker without a hoot and a holler. Whit ground his teeth and swallowed a growl.

She ate quicker than a coyote, swept everyone's plates away and into the sink, and left Buck with his mouth full and a fork in his hand. When she came back and snatched the fork, Baker laughed outright and shoved away from the table.

Livvy faced them all with her hands on her hips, ready to shame each and every one of them. "Who will be gathering eggs tomorrow morning?" Whit jerked a thumb at Buck, who couldn't speak for himself.

"He will."

Baker hooted again.

"Buck, use this basket." She pushed it to the end of the counter. "And let that old red hen alone. She's setting and we need some hatchlings this summer. Besides, she'll peck a hole in your hand if you try to move her."

By the glint in her eye, Whit knew Livvy was toying with the boy, but Buck didn't. He nearly choked on his biscuit and quickly downed the last of his coffee.

"Yes, ma'am."

Livvy peeled soap into the dishpan and informed everyone and no one in particular that deer had gotten into the garden again last night. "If you all want any more greens—or rhubarb pie, for that matter—you'll be needing to fix the fence."

"Deer don't eat rhubarb." Whit's ma had told him that years ago. Said the leaves made them sick.

"Tell that to the deer." Livvy cast a blue light over her shoulder and he nearly squinted in the brilliance.

He grabbed his hat and stormed out the door before he shamed himself by begging her not to go.

Infuriating woman.

Bess dozed in the traces and Whit checked her harness just to have something to do. He'd already greased the axles and made sure the wheels were sound. Livvy didn't need to break down between the ranch and town. She didn't need to ride off alone at all. He'd get Baker to listen to reason.

And then the woman flew out the back door with her

bonnet and satchel and a look in her eye that warned him not to get in her way. Like a green-broke colt.

"I'll be back by noon tomorrow." Livvy set her satchel in the back, hiked her skirt with one hand and held out the other hand to Whit.

He took it and grasped her elbow as she climbed the wheel. She settled onto the seat, spread her skirt about her feet and gathered the reins.

"Be careful." He swallowed the kiss he wanted to give her. "Don't let her run with you."

Livvy rewarded him with a true smile. She leaned over and laid her hand against his cheek. Quickly he covered it with his own.

"I will be fine, Whitaker Hutton. You take care of my grandfather while I'm gone."

He turned his head and kissed her palm, heard the catch in her breath, and reluctantly let her pull her hand away. The bonnet hid her face, but when she flicked the reins she glanced his way, washing him in a blue gaze that set his insides afire.

"Giddyap, Bess."

Like a lost pup, he stood in the yard and watched her drive away. *Lord, keep her safe.*

The back door shut and Whit turned to see Baker lumber over, hat in his hand. He slapped it on his head, stopped a few paces away and leveled a hard eye on Whit. "You thinkin' about puttin' your brand on her?"

Surprised by his boss's question, Whit hesitated to tell the man he was in love with his granddaughter. But he was. That was the truth of the matter, and he might as well face the old bull head-on.

He straightened his shoulders, stood squarely on both feet. "Yes, sir, I am."

Baker's silver mustache twitched at one end and he

jerked his head in a sideways nod. "'Bout time." Then he hobbled off toward the barn.

If Whit's horse had talked to him, he could not have been more surprised. Those words constituted a blessing.

Joy split his insides and he could feel his face cracking in a Buck grin. He wanted to whoop. He wanted to jump on Oro and catch Livvy and ask her to marry him and kiss her good right there on the wagon seat.

A sudden, sober thought punctured his happiness. He screwed his hat down and headed for the barn. Any woman wanted her father's blessing, as well. Could he afford to ride to Denver to ask the Reverend Hartman for his daughter's hand? And what did he have to show for himself—a foreman's salary, a good horse and a saddle? Not much for a gal who deserved a whole lot more.

Suddenly the morning light glared harsh and unforgiving.

How would he ever get Olivia Hartman to be his bride?

Livvy's left hand burned as sure as a yearling's hide. She turned it over and was surprised to see no seared brand smoking in her white palm. Whit Hutton had kissed her hand. *Her hand!* Not like an English gentleman dips his head to a lady's gloved fingers. But...*intimately.*

Shivers ran up her back and she slapped Bess into a trot. If she had to take an easy walk the entire ten miles to town, she'd surely jump out of her skin.

What she wouldn't give for a moment with Mama Ruth. Her grandmother would know what it felt like to be swept away by a cowboy's charms.

A bouncing laugh escaped her throat as Bess clopped merrily along the ranch road. Her grade-school teacher would qualify *cowboy's charms* as an oxymoron. But Livvy knew better. The two words fit together like bacon and beans, and they came in the shape of one Whitaker Hutton.

The kiss wasn't his first gentle tenderness. She thought of that day in the columbines, the moments beneath the slicker in the hailstorm. Even his roughly insistent offer of the gloves and canteen showed his concern. Somehow those small tokens had swept away every barb he'd ever thrown at her. She clucked her tongue and flicked the reins.

What might it feel like to really kiss him? She shivered and pushed her bonnet back, let the sun do the kissing.

The sky spread strikingly blue above Fremont Peak and the lesser hills that guarded the gorge where men fought over the right-of-way. She sobered at the thought of Tad and Jody getting mixed up in the so-called war. Whit would never do such a thing.

Doubt wiggled beneath her breastbone and she pressed a hand against it, forbidding it to spread. Whit was too levelheaded, too smart to be caught in a foolish fight over a railway.

As she neared the bend that turned sharply along the river and into town, cottonwood trees waved a shimmering greeting. The Arkansas rushed at their feet, shouting to be heard above Bess's hoofbeats. Children played outside the hotel across the river, and couples strolled hand in hand along the footbridge dangling mere inches above the swollen river. She drove by the massive stone wall of the territorial prison and passed carriages and lone horseback riders headed to the hot springs. Mules pulled by with freighters' heavy wagons bound for the mining camps. What would happen to those supply wagons and the men who drove them once the railroad won passage through the mountains to Leadville?

The number of people increased as she drove farther into town, but this time she sat proudly with her best bonnet and Sunday shoes. She might not have a parasol, or even the latest, most fashionable dress, but contentment spread across her heart and she sat a little straighter. She had a pair of britches and could hold her own with a branding iron. She doubted that any fine women she saw on the boardwalks could say as much.

At the church she turned Bess into the lane and the mare quickened her pace for the secondary home and hay crib ahead. Livvy pulled into the yard behind the parsonage, where Whit's mother knelt weeding the columbines that edged the porch. Annie stood and pressed her hands against her lower back, then shook out her skirt and greeted Livvy with a bright smile.

"Welcome!" She extended a hand as Livvy climbed down and then enfolded her in a warm hug. "It's so good to see you again, and so soon." Her brow knit together and she stepped aside to peek in the wagon. "Oh," she breathed. "I was afraid you had another wounded young man with you. This train war has gotten completely out of hand."

Livvy's shoulders relaxed at Annie's welcome. "No wounded men, only my satchel in case…" She hesitated and looked down at her hands, not knowing exactly how to phrase her request without begging or sounding presumptuous.

"Oh, by all means, you must stay the night." Annie's deep copper eyes twinkled with comprehension and the arm she linked through Livvy's confirmed her sincerity. "I can't tell you how much Marti and I could use a good woman-to-woman visit."

"Thank you so much. I need a few supplies from the mercantile and I'd hoped I wouldn't be an imposition."

"You must always think of us as an open home. Come in, come in."

Arm in arm they headed for the shady back porch, where Annie halted suddenly on the lowest step. "Did you come alone?"

Livvy hated to disappoint the woman, aware that Annie would love to see her only son. "Yes, I'm sorry. Whit is busy at the ranch."

Annie snorted—a most shocking reaction that Livvy surprisingly adored in this lovely woman.

"He is a man now and can't be chasing off to visit his mother."

Livvy's palm warmed again with Whit's send-off. "I believe he wanted to come, but Pop won out. I think giving me a day to do as I please was his way of thanking me for my help with the branding."

Annie opened the door to the kitchen and a question danced in her eyes. "You helped with the branding? You mean you cooked?"

Livvy untied her bonnet strings and laid the light cotton cover on the table. "Yes, I cooked, but I did that at the house. I helped *brand*. I ran the iron, as they say."

Annie's head wagged as she pumped water into a teakettle and set it on the stove. "My, but you do have pluck, young lady. It sounds like those men are working you to the bone."

Livvy settled into a chair at the table. "I loved it. Really. It was so exciting to ride again and help gather the cattle." She shivered slightly as she remembered her near wreck on Ranger.

"Surely you didn't do all that in a skirt?" The way Annie said it made Livvy want to snort herself.

"I wore my grandmother's denims."

Annie joined her at the table while the water heated. "That sounds absolutely wonderful. I am nearly jealous of your adventure."

The front door opened and someone entered through the parlor with a cheery "I'm home." Ruddy cheeked and exuding unbridled energy, Martha Hutton rushed into the kitchen with a stack of papers and books. She dropped them on the table and fell into a chair.

"Oh—Livvy. Did my beastly brother chase you off?"

"Marti!" Annie reddened at her spirited daughter's outburst.

"Oh, Mama, you know I'm only joking."

"Ladies do not joke, Martha Mae."

Livvy stifled a laugh and gave Marti a teasing frown. "You know, we will have to discuss that. Sometimes I could absolutely whack him with a carpet beater."

Marti leaned back in her chair and laughed remarkably like her brother. Shaking her head, Annie rose to attend to the water and bring cups to the table.

After a lively visit, Annie went to the henhouse to choose a young fryer for dinner. Livvy made herself useful by scrubbing and peeling potatoes for a salad, only too happy to be busy. Marti set half a dozen eggs in a small pot on the stove.

"You're going to think I'm terrible, but I hope Mother doesn't call me out to help her wring that chicken's neck. I can't stand to do that." The girl shuddered and her fiery red curls shook in agreement.

How would Marti survive on a ranch? Livvy glanced at the books on the table. "Are those papers last term's school studies?"

Marti brightened. "Oh, no." She swiped her hands down her white apron, drying them front and back from the egg water that had splashed them. "These are library books and the papers are notes I took at Mr. Winton's museum this morning." She sat down at the table and spread out the papers.

"Really it's just a curio shop next door to the saloon, but some people have recently been referring to Winton's collection as a museum. Two years ago he had an absolutely marvelous display there of fossils uncovered at the Finch ranch dig."

Livvy frowned. "A dig?"

"Yes, a paleontological dig." Marti's voice assumed a dignified tone as she enunciated the foreign-sounding word. "Our school superintendent has been excavating near Garden Park for quite some time and has uncovered the most amazing dinosaur bones."

Livvy's newspaper hat lining came to mind.

"Two years ago they hauled off five wagonloads of fossils all believed to come from the same animal. Can you imagine anything so large?"

Livvy caught the glow on Marti's face as the girl shuffled through her notes.

"Where did the wagons go?"

Marti paused in her rearranging and looked at Livvy in apparent surprise. "Why, to the Academy of Natural Sciences in Philadelphia, of course."

Of course.

Marti spit out a most unladylike huff. "Papa wants me to go to school to be a teacher, but I want to be a paleontologist. It sounds ever so much more exciting."

"Well, at least those animals would have no blood or feathers to contend with."

The girl sucked in a quick breath and burst out in that hearty Hutton laughter. "Oh, Livvy, you are so right!"

The back door opened and Annie stuck her head inside. "I need your help with the feathers, Marti. Bring a bowl we can drop them in to wash later."

If Marti had been a balloon she could not have deflated any quicker or more completely. Casting a remorseful eye at Livvy, she rose and took a bowl from the sideboard with all the excitement of a funeral procession. "Coming, Mother."

Livvy adjusted the damper and set the potatoes on to

cook. Martha's parents wanted her to be a schoolteacher. Livvy's wanted her to be a nurse. Did the Huttons want Whit to be a preacher like his father, or a storekeeper like his grandfather?

She let out a heavy sigh. No one asked *them* what they wanted to do with their lives.

With the eggs and potatoes cooking, Livvy dried her hands on a towel and poured herself more tea. At the table she added a heaping spoon of sugar from the double-handled bowl. Tarnished by daily use, the old silver relic boasted a dull patina rather than a shiny polished exterior. A well-used dinosaur.

Livvy assuaged her guilt at not volunteering to pluck feathers by setting the table for four and hunting down a jar of pickled cucumbers to cut into the potato salad. When Marti returned from her most dreaded chore, she washed her hands and arms at the sink and splashed water on her face.

"Would you like to go with me to the mercantile for supplies?" Livvy said. "We could even stop by the curio shop and you could show me Mr. Winton's bones."

The girl perked up immediately and yanked off her apron. "They're not Mr. Winton's bones. He's not even dead yet."

Livvy laughed. "Oh, Marti, where did you get your delightful sense of humor?" She set her half-finished tea on the counter and picked up her bonnet.

Marti ran upstairs and back down before Livvy made it out to the porch.

"I'm running errands with Livvy, Mama. Any messages for Grandma and Grandpa?"

Livvy watched Annie's face for disapproval of her daughter's quick escape but instead found the usual sparkle in her eyes. "Yes. Tell them I love them and to come for supper tomorrow."

Marti bounded into the wagon seat.

Annie's head wagged again. She dangled a quite naked and headless bird in one hand and pushed graying strays from her temple with the other. "I don't know what I'm going to do with that child." She gave Livvy an encouraging look. "Maybe your housekeeping and cooking sense will rub off on her. I daresay mine hasn't made much impact."

Livvy climbed up next to the girl, and with a parting wave, turned Bess down the short lane to Main Street.

Even her parents' home wasn't so close to the markets. But Denver was so much larger than Cañon City. A body couldn't live this close to downtown unless they took a room above a storefront or moved into a rooming house. Livvy shuddered. Living that close to so many people and so much noise? How could she ever?

Visions of purple columbines bobbed into her thoughts, whispering their secrets in the cool aspen shade. The palm of her hand warmed around Bess's reins and Livvy tried to measure which was softer—the mountain flower's delicate petals or a certain cowboy's kiss.

"You passed the mercantile."

Marti's voice jerked Livvy from her high meadow and back to Cañon City. "Yes." Daydreaming could land them at the opposite end of town. "We will come back after the museum."

"Oh, good." The girl straightened and pointed ahead on the right. "Just ahead in the next block, this side of the saloon."

Wonderful. Livvy was escorting the preacher's daughter into the neighborhood of the saloon. Lord, help them.

Chapter 15

Whit's imposed day of rest for everyone nearly drove him crazy. Without something to do he'd be loco by noon, and cutting hay wasn't his idea of a good distraction.

Two colts waited in the near pasture. He could run them into the corral at the barn and start working with them. His gut told him that wasn't a good idea, either, not with the way his thoughts kept wandering off after Livvy and the buckboard.

But he'd for certain lose his mind soaping saddles, mending tack or helping Buck repair the garden fence. He watched the boy wrestle with the newfangled barbed wire that Baker wanted strung in a double row above the top rail. It sure enough lived up to its name—the devil's rope—with those spiny points laced into the wire.

Whit hunted for Baker and found him in the barn resetting a shoe on Ranger. As Whit walked up, his boss let the horse's back left hoof slide off his leather apron and stood straight. Stooping over didn't seem to bother the man as long as he didn't have to bend his right leg.

"I'm riding up to Overton's, see if she needs help with her chores."

Baker dropped his hammer in a small wooden box, unbuckled the apron and hung it on a nail. "Tell her we'll come brand her calves in the next few days. See if she has irons. If not, I'm sure Buck can work out her brand with the rings."

Whit nodded and turned on his heel, not interested in conversation or in explaining his jittery condition to the steely-eyed Baker. He saddled Oro, swung up and struck out for the widow's, six miles west as the creek ran.

And the creek was more than runnin'. The usually clear stream gushed across the meadow. Muddy with mountain storm water, it swamped its banks like syrup on hotcakes. Oro pranced across, tucking his chin and twitching his ears at the chattering late-spring runoff. Yesterday's storm had hurried the high-country snowmelt and most likely set the Arkansas to churning.

Not any more than Whit's gut. That little catch in Livvy's breath when he kissed her hand had spurred his heartbeat as sure as any Mexican rowel set a bronc to twisting. And she'd not jerked away. From the look on her face, she'd liked it. But that didn't solve his problem of getting her father's blessing and having something to show for his own worth.

He should have bought those cows when he was thinking about it instead of chewing on the matter. Three, four head even. Anything was better than nothing.

Whit rode over a draw in the near hills and paused to look down on the Overton place. The woman still lived in the tent her husband had put up. An unfinished cabin slouched next to it. Another winter like the last one and she and her no-account son might freeze to death.

Whit took the trail down in plain view of the camp and waved his hat over his head, hoping the widow would see the movement if she didn't hear him coming. He didn't need a startled woman peppering him and his horse with buckshot or bullets.

She stooped over a campfire tripod stirring something in an iron kettle. Supper, he supposed. Beans and a little pork wafted toward him. She set the spoon aside, returned the lid and straightened. As he reined up next to the half-built cabin, Whit could easily see the worry lines that creased a face too young to look that old.

Would that happen to Livvy if she married him?

The thought cut him like a barb on Buck's new garden wire.

The widow pushed hair off her face with the back of her hand. "Good morning, Whit. What brings you over?"

He stepped off Oro and ground tied him, then he took his hat off and walked to the fire. "Mornin', ma'am."

She handed him a tin cup of strong-smelling coffee. He nodded his thanks and sat on an upturned stump. She took a stump opposite with the tripod between them and cradled a similar cup. Even from a distance her hands revealed the rough cracked skin of hard work.

"I've come to see if you need any help with your chores." He glanced around for some sign of what needed to be done.

The woman looked over her shoulder at the tent then returned her attention to Whit. "We're doing all right. Tad's been getting stronger every day, but he's resting now. Takes it out of him in the mornings."

The tent flap pulled back and the boy stepped out, his arm in a sling and his hair dirty and wild like a mountain man's. Gaunt and weary, he lowered himself onto a stump and his mother handed him her coffee.

Surprised to see Tad back so soon, a knot yanked into

Whit's gut. The odds were against these two. Sure, he and Buck could finish the Overtons' cabin before winter, but would the widow and her boy get enough food stored up? Did they have warm clothes and enough ammunition to keep varmints away?

Did they have any money for supplies?

An old buckboard sat behind the tent and two horses grazed a ways off.

"We're makin' out." The boy's defiant tone made Whit think otherwise.

"How many head do you have?" Whit swirled the thick coffee, watched it lap around the inside of the cup rather than catch the boy's eye and get his back up.

"Twenty," the widow said. "Twenty cows. At least that's how many my husband bought." She looked down at her hands and the hair fell back across her tired eyes.

"You be interested in selling them?" Whit spooked himself with the question, wondering how it had fallen out of his mouth without so much as a serious consideration.

Mother and son exchanged a look and she sat a little straighter, pushed her hair back again.

"You offering?" the boy asked.

Was he? Baker had tried to buy her out in early spring, but she'd refused. Had loneliness, backbreaking work and the boy's stupidity changed her mind? Whit made an offer—every last dollar he had in his bedroll.

The boy looked at his mother and she jerked a nod.

"Done." Tad rose and walked to Whit and stuck his left hand out in a backward handshake. "They're yours."

Whit stood and took the boy's hand but kept his eyes on Mrs. Overton. The cattle were more hers than her son's. The transaction was hers to make.

She looked at Whit. "You can have the land, too, for another hundred."

Whit didn't have another hundred and wasn't sure he

wanted the place. Things were getting outta hand. Helping with the Overtons' chores was a lot different than buying the whole kit and caboodle.

"I'll see what I can do." Again his gut knotted. See what he could do? He'd already done too much.

She sighed and a few worry lines slipped off her face. Whit looked again to make certain, and sure enough, she seemed ten years younger already. She almost smiled.

"We can be out tomorrow. Can you get the money by then?"

She didn't beat around the bush any more than Livvy.

"There's no hurry, ma'am. You can take your time. I might not be able to get back over here tomorrow."

Her shoulders slumped and she shrank before his eyes. Tad coughed and wiped his mouth on his dirty sleeve. "Doc Mason told me he needed a nurse, or someone who could help him with his patients. I told him Ma here was right good with fixin' people and he said he'd think on it. We could sure use that job 'fore somebody beats us to it."

We? Us? Whit wanted to thrash the boy. "What will you be doing while your ma's working for the doctor? Taking potshots at the railroad crew?"

Whit's conscience barely nipped him as a scowl curled Tad's brow into a dark snake. With a bold stare, Whit dared the boy to make something of the remark. He'd gladly give him the lickin' he needed.

"We'll be ready when you come with the money." Mrs. Overton stood and Whit heard goodbye in the movement. He handed her his coffee cup and put on his hat. But Tad wasn't finished.

"I ain't the only one worked on the rail lines." He smirked as if his information was valuable. Whit took the bait.

"Is that right? Someone from around here?" Suddenly Jody galloped through his thoughts.

"You missin' a hand over at Baker's spread?"

Whit took a step toward the boy. "You know something you should be tellin' me?"

The smirk held but Tad moved behind the stump. "Jody Perkins rode through here three days ago, first day I was back. Said he was gonna lay rail."

"Hush, Tad. You don't know if he really went to work for the railroad. He could have been full of bluster."

Tad snorted and hung the thumb on his good hand in his waist. "He's there. Makin' three dollars a day at it. A whole lot better'n punchin' cows."

Whit wanted to wipe the sneer off the boy's face but he figured he'd have a she-bear on his back if he tried it. He shoved his hat down hard and looked at Mrs. Overton. "I'll be back tomorrow."

Curious, indeed. Livvy looked at the sign above the store as they left: Winton's Curiosity Shop. She had read about prehistoric creatures once roaming the earth, had even seen drawings of their massive bones the size of a man. But to see one right before her eyes was an experience she'd never dreamed of. In a small way, she understood Marti's fascination with the unusual and her rejection of the mundane.

Not that teaching children was mundane. It was honorable work for any woman. But studying fossils and discovering secrets of the past offered the mystique of the unknown.

She drove Bess around the corner, two blocks east and back to Main Street, where they stopped at the rail before Whitaker's Mercantile. Marti jumped down with a young boy's enthusiasm rather than a lady's grace and restraint. No wonder Annie Hutton had fits over her daughter.

The girl dashed through the door, setting the bell to singing as she raised her own melodic "Hel-lo-oh."

Livvy set the brake, looped the reins and followed Marti

through the open door. The smells swept her back to childhood days of visiting her grandparents and stopping here
for a sweet. And Mr. Whitaker looked the same, with
his snowy hair and mustache and rosy Father Christmas
cheeks. Marti greeted him with a kiss and a hug, then hurried to the back, where her grandmother Martha ground
fresh coffee beans. Arbuckle's, Livvy guessed from the
rich aroma. Mentally she added several pounds to her list.

Livvy held her hand out to Mr. Whitaker. "Good day,
sir. How nice to see you again after so long."

He smothered her hand in both of his and cocked one
white brow. "It's Daniel to you, young lady. Why, you're
nearly kin, you know."

Feeling as much, she warmed in his welcome. "I feel
the same, Daniel. Thank you." Withdrawing her hand, she
turned to survey the goods and stopped at the sight of the
bright flag that hung on the store's back wall—new since
her last visit. Thirty-eight white stars gleamed against a
deep blue field, flanked on the right and below by white
and red stripes.

"Is this the first time you've been down since Colorado
joined the union?" he said.

Livvy tallied the years. "The first time I've been in the
mercantile. The last time we came was for Mama Ruth's
services. We didn't stop in then."

A sudden sadness flickered in the man's eyes. "So sorry
to lose her, dear. So sorry."

He patted his ample stomach and came around the counter. "Well, now, you must be here for supplies. I understand you are helping your grandfather Baker at the ranch."

"Yes." She reached in her skirt pocket for the list.

"Did Whit ride in with you?"

Against Livvy's deepest wishes, warmth raced up her
neck and into her face. She turned away, suddenly interested in the nesting salt boxes against the opposite wall.

"Not this time. He had too much work." She bit her mouth at the near lie, trying to assure herself it was partially true.

A deep chuckle rumbled in the man's chest and she suspected Daniel Whitaker saw through most of his customers' defenses. "I was hoping the boy would take over the store for Martha and me, but he's set on cowboying."

Daniel laughed. "His father was the same way. He wasn't always a preacher, you know."

Livvy did not know. *That* story had not made it to the dinner table. "No, I have not heard about Pastor Hutton's younger days." She faced the storekeeper, hoping to learn more.

Instead, Daniel held out his hand for her list.

"I will also have five pounds of that wonderful Arbuckle's I smell cooking," she said.

"I married a mighty smart woman." He glanced at Martha and her namesake, their heads bent together over some intriguing topic. "We've sold more coffee since she keeps it going all day instead of only in the morning. People can't resist the smell."

Within an hour, Livvy had her flour and sugar, coffee and toweling, and a few other things not on her list that she knew her grandfather wouldn't mind. Daniel had the wagon loaded, and she stood at the counter as he wrote out her ticket.

"In a way, I'm glad Whit did not come to town with you."

Livvy caught his quick glance.

He pulled letters from her grandfather's mail slot, handed them to her and lowered his voice. "There's going to be trouble over that railroad." He leaned across the counter and dropped to a whisper. "Santa Fe hired a Kansas sheriff to come head the fight and got the U.S. marshal's office to pin a star on him."

Livvy blinked and held her breath.

"Bat Masterson. A fast gun, they say. He brought in his pal J. H. Holliday to gather a posse of sorts, and they're holed up at the roundhouse in Pueblo."

The hushed urgency in the man's voice chilled Livvy's blood no less that the mountain lion's scream. "Why are you telling me this?" The hand holding the mail trembled. Daniel enfolded it in his.

"I'm sorry, Livvy, darlin'. I didn't mean to frighten you, but I know you are a praying gal. Both you and Whit were raised by godly parents, and you could not do any better than to pray that this so-called war comes to a halt."

His bushy brows locked together. "If it comes to a fight, it's not the wealthy train barons that will be catching lead. It's the young men from this community."

Livvy forced herself to breathe.

Chapter 16

Whit opened the kitchen door and sucked in a hoot that nearly knocked him over. Baker stood at the stove flipping hotcakes, Livvy's apron tied high around his chest.

"Mornin'." Whit coughed heartily as he stepped inside and hung his hat on a chair.

Baker scowled over his shoulder. "Least you didn't say *good* mornin'." He poured a saucer-size round of batter and picked up the coffeepot with a bandanna to protect his hand. "Coffee's hot. Buck's out pickin' eggs." He snorted. "Livvy's got him plumb scared of that red hen."

Whit marveled at Livvy's ability to keep them all doing her bidding. And missing her like a pup missed its ma. He held a cup out. "Thanks."

Baker returned to the griddle. "What'd you learn at Overton's?"

Whit swallowed a mouthful and flinched. A bit stouter than what Livvy cooked up. "The widow wants to sell."

Baker plated the cake onto a stack next to the stove,

shoved the griddle back and took the plate to the table. "Grab the molasses."

Whit found a tin on the sideboard, and tucked into the corner, a jar of his mother's apple butter. He brought it, too. Served Livvy right if they ate it all while she was gone, leaving them the way she had.

Feeling all of twelve years old, he set the jar and tin on the table and took a seat.

Baker forked three cakes onto his plate and doused them with molasses. "How many head does she have?"

Confession was good for the soul, Whit's pa had always said. "None."

Baker looked up.

"I bought every blasted one, sight unseen." Whit slumped beneath the weight of what he'd done. He'd have to work for Baker another four years just to earn back what he'd spent in less than four minutes.

Baker grunted, cut into his hotcakes. "How many?"

"Says there's twenty cows but could be forty head by now, counting yearlings and older calves. Don't even know if they've been branded."

Baker sopped up a mouthful and chewed for a moment. "That will get you started. You gonna run 'em with mine?"

"I'd like to. Been thinking on a brand but I haven't registered one yet."

Baker watched him with that gunmetal glare. Whit wasn't about to tell him of his idea—a double H for Hutton and Hartman beneath the mountain peak. He had to tell Livvy first, that was, if her father allowed the union. The thought soured even his mother's sweet apple butter dripping off his hotcakes.

"You takin' the land, too?"

"Can't." Whit forked another bite and followed it with coffee. "She wants a hundred dollars for it."

Baker pushed his plate back and picked up his cup. "They prove it up yet?"

"Started a cabin, but it's not half-finished. She's still living in a tent."

Baker grunted, swirled his coffee. "I'll stake you."

Whit sucked air and coughed until he thought he'd lose his hotcakes. He swabbed his face with his neckerchief and downed the rest of his coffee.

"Don't choke up on me, son." Baker's mustache quivered on one side, a sure sign of pleasure in his joke. "You can pay me back in calves. Take you a few years, but it'll work out."

"Thank you, sir." Whit's thoughts swam around like panicky cows fording a swollen river.

"Overton's land borders mine, doesn't it?"

"Yes, sir."

"Good. That will make it easier. When will you take her the money?"

Whit sat straighter, tried to stretch out his lungs, open his burning throat. "Today. She was in a hurry to leave. Has an offer from Doc Mason, Tad said—he's back home already. Said Doc needs help and his ma's handy at fixin' folks. Other than bullet wounds, I suppose. Anyway, she said they'd be packed and ready to leave when I showed up."

Baker shoved his chair back. "If her cattle are close, drive them back over the draw and run 'em in with our bunch. That might keep rustlers off them."

"There's one other thing."

Baker stilled.

"Tad said Jody rode through their place three days ago. Said he was gonna sign on to lay rail for the Santa Fe."

Baker rolled a couple of words around under his breath and snatched his plate off the table.

"I want to go get him." Whit waited for his boss to break

in half over that piece of news, but the man held his tongue and set his dishes in the sink. He jerked off Livvy's apron and faced Whit.

"Don't get yourself shot."

Whit took his plate and cup to the counter. "There isn't anybody else to bring him home. No family other than Buck and us, and with Buck's luck, he'd get his head blown off if he showed up down in the gorge."

Baker turned for the dining room. "Come by my study before you leave, and I'll give you the money for the widow."

"Thank you, sir."

The back door flew open and Buck lurched in with a basket full of eggs and a bloody hand. "That fool chicken attacked me!"

Baker shook his head and lumbered into the dining room.

"Boil some water and wash the dishes. It'll clean out your hand. And give me those before you drop 'em." Whit grabbed the basket. The eggs were still warm.

"But I'm starving."

Whit jerked his chin toward the table and the remaining cold cakes. "You can have what's left."

Whit set the eggs on a towel the way he'd seen Livvy do. He took a napkin from the counter and on his way past the table snatched a hotcake and rolled it up for the ride.

"Hey!" Buck's offended tone rankled.

"That's what you get for messing with that hen when Livvy told you not to."

Four cold cakes and what was left of the apple butter should hold the boy. If Whit remembered right, Ma had given Livvy *two* jars. He'd look for the other one when he returned with Jody.

At the bunkhouse, Whit stuffed his savings in his waistcoat, strapped on his gun belt and picked up his rifle and scabbard. He didn't intend to join the fight, but no sense being foolhardy and unprotected. Sometimes looking well-heeled kept the roughs off your back. He hoped for as much today.

He led the buckskin to the hitching rail in front of the house and out of habit, peered at the lace window curtains. No white square tipped him off to Livvy's attempt at secrecy. Pressure built up behind his ribs and he pulled deeply on the clean, morning air. He'd find her some columbines, help her plant 'em by the back door. Like his pa had for his mother.

He jerked his hat off and scrubbed his head, digging deep for his brain. What was he thinking? This wasn't his place. And what kind of cowhand went around digging posies?

He stomped his boots on the landing and stepped inside. Baker sat at his desk in the small study off the dining room, opposite the front door.

"Come on back." The man opened a drawer and withdrew a small wooden box.

As Whit approached the large walnut desk, he noted the intricate floral pattern carved into the box lid. Must have been Ruth Baker's. What was it with women and flowers?

Baker withdrew the money and returned the box to its place. Then he folded the bill in half and handed it to Whit. "You going to Texas Creek after Overton's?"

"Yes, sir. Should take me half a day to get up there and haul him back. Then we can push the widow's cows over the draw on our return." He tucked the bill in with the rest of his money.

"Buck and I can handle things while you're gone." Baker narrowed his eyes at Whit. "You tell him what you're doing?"

"No, sir."

Baker jerked his head in quick agreement.

Whit hesitated.

"What?"

"If Jody's not where I think he is, at that rock fort, I'm gonna hunt for him. He could be someplace else along the river."

"Face down."

A muscle in Whit's cheek flinched. He truly hoped the boy hadn't gotten himself killed.

Baker waved his hand in dismissal. "Don't get shot." He leaned back in his leather chair, both hands grasping the worn armrests. "I don't think Olivia could take it."

Whit's neck warmed beneath his collar and he flicked a look at the man's eyes. All of a sudden he knew why Baker was staking him on the Overton place.

Livvy thought sure a good night's rest would soothe her ragged nerves, but that required sleep and she got precious little of it.

As soon as dawn pinked the sky, she rose, bathed at the wash basin and stepped into her petticoat and dress. She scrubbed her teeth with a small brush and baking soda mix from a tin in her satchel, then rebraided her hair and twisted it low at her neck. Buttoning her good shoes with a hook, she regretted not wearing her boots instead. Less trouble.

She repacked her satchel and smoothed the star quilt, wishing she could smooth away her worry over Whit as easily. She eased the bedroom door open. Marti's door was closed, but her parents' door stood slightly ajar. A light glowed at the bottom of the stairway, and Livvy suspected Annie was making biscuits or gathering eggs.

She crept down the stairs and stopped near the bottom. Annie sat at the kitchen table with a lamp drawn near and a Bible opened before her. Her forehead rested against her two opened hands and her lips moved. Feeling intrusive,

Livvy grasped the railing and stepped up to the previous stair, catching her skirt in the process. Her petticoat ripped, she gasped, and Annie looked up.

"Good morning." Annie rose and came toward the stairs. "I see you are an early riser, too."

"I am sorry to disturb you."

Annie reached for the satchel. "You are not bothering me in the least. I was merely starting the day the way I always do—with the Lord." She set the satchel by the back door and went to the stove, where coffee simmered. "Want a cup?"

"Yes, thank you." Livvy took a chair at the table and looked to see what Scripture Annie was reading. Proverbs 3.

"Trust in the Lord with all thine heart; and lean not unto thine own understanding." Annie poured two cups as she recited the verse and brought them to the table with two spoons.

"You know it by memory." Livvy wilted at the stab of guilt for not being more familiar with the Scriptures. And she, a preacher's daughter.

Annie seated herself and reached for the silver sugar bowl. "That is exactly the reason. Those words go straight to my heart every time I read them. And when I need the Lord's comfort and strength, reciting them is the quickest and shortest route I know."

Livvy waited until Annie had sugared her coffee before dipping her spoon into the bowl. "I haven't spent the time reading that I should, at least not since coming to help Pop at the ranch. It seems like every waking moment is spent cooking or cleaning or gathering or washing. Some household chore always needs tending to."

"Or branding?" Annie's eyes sparkled with mirth.

Livvy muted a laugh with her hand. "Oh, yes, branding. And dare I admit I liked it better than most any other chore?" Because it put her close to Whit.

"I can't say I blame you, though I'm sure my hands would suffer from such a task."

Livvy felt a certain affinity with Annie, one she believed she could trust. "Whit gave me sturdy leather gloves to use. I think they were once his." She dared not meet Annie's gaze, affinity or not.

"Hmm. I am not surprised that he looks after you like that. I saw his affection for you when you were here last."

Livvy stole a quick glance to see if Annie meant those revealing words. Who knew a man better than his mother?

Annie gave her a knowing smile. "He cares for you, I am certain. May I be so bold as to ask if you feel the same?"

Livvy should have let the sun scorch her face yesterday on the way to town. Better that than its current competition with the brightening dawn burning through the windows.

"Yes, I do." So faint was her answer she doubted if Annie heard it.

The woman reached out to grasp Livvy's hand. "That does me good to hear, Livvy. I have been praying for you both." Annie rose and set about starting breakfast.

Livvy felt as obvious as a thistle in a columbine patch, certain her cheeks were just as brilliant. But hearing that Whit's mother prayed for her—for them—touched something deep in her soul.

The hot coffee was warming her more than necessary. She picked up the egg basket. "I'll gather for you this morning. Is the coop behind the barn?"

"Yes, dear. Attached on the left side. Two hens are setting. A red and a black-and-white speckled."

Livvy thought of her grandfather's surly russet hen and wondered if Buck had survived the chore.

Later at breakfast, all the Huttons were in a better mood than the previous night when Livvy had asked her unfortunate questions: Which side was in the right regarding the railroad war? And was the whole thing really worth dying over? Marti had fled from the table and remained in her room the rest of the evening.

Undoubtedly, the display had something to do with young Tad Overton, for Pastor Hutton had raked his brows together and made a guttural sound just like Whit. Livvy had shuddered.

But in the light of morning, Marti sat at the table with swollen eyes that quickly brightened as she told her parents about Livvy's first visit to the curio shop. The girl's obvious delight in fossil remains pulled her toward a scholarly pursuit, though not the scholarly pursuit her parents imagined. However, if it drew her affections away from the Overton boy, Livvy guessed her family might accept it.

Eager to be on her way, Livvy folded her napkin and gathered her plate and cup. "Thank you for breakfast, Annie. And for supper last night and your wonderful company, all of you." She looked to each one to emphasize her sincerity.

"Maybe you can persuade our son to come with you next time." The pastor held his coffee mug in both hands, elbows resting on the table like Whit. Livvy's chest tightened.

"I will try." She smiled, hoping it masked her worry over Whit's uncommon sense of duty where the Perkins boys were concerned.

"And remind him that Papa Whitaker wants him to take over the mercantile." Marti tacked on the afterthought with a dash of sibling impishness. Livvy looked away to hide a grin. And a jealous tug. She did not want to marry a store clerk. She wanted to marry a cowboy. A *particular* cowboy.

Oh, Lord, how self-centered she was.

"Do you have any idea how early Doc Mason is up and around?" Livvy picked up her satchel and stood by the door.

Annie brought two jars from her pantry, wrapped them in toweling and tucked them into the dark leather bag. "It always depends on how late his last call was the day before. But don't mind knocking on his door. If he doesn't answer, you will simply have to come back to town."

Livvy pushed the jars deeper into her satchel. "Thank you for the—apple butter?"

Annie nodded. "Of course."

"I left one jar out for the men while I was gone, hoping to appease them in my absence."

Annie gave Livvy a light kiss on the cheek. "You are a good woman, Livvy Hartman."

Marti rose and took Livvy's hand. "Come back soon and we can go to the library. They have books on paleontology. And if you stay long enough, we could take the buggy up to the quarry to see the dig."

"Perhaps, Marti. Don't make rash promises." Her father's remark dampened the girl's spirit only briefly, and she shot Livvy a sly wink and quick nod.

Outside by the columbines, Livvy paused for one last look. "Thank you all again. I will be sure to give Whit your best wishes."

"You could give him a big kiss, too."

Annie's quick swat nearly knocked her daughter off the porch. Livvy was grateful she had turned toward the wagon and was climbing aboard with the pastor's hand at her elbow as he steadied her ascent. His half-hitched smile reaffirmed the Hutton family's playful spirit.

Livvy settled the satchel at her feet and clucked Bess ahead. With a quick slap of the ribbons she was on her way down the lane and onto Main Street. One stop at Doc Mason's, and then home. She should be at the ranch well before noon, within three hours at the most if she hurried.

And her heart said to hurry.

Chapter 17

Whit rode into the camp at a slow walk.

True to her word, the widow had all her worldly possessions—which wasn't much—loaded in the old buckboard and a sorry-looking horse hitched to it. The other horse was tied to the back. She and Tad waited on stumps around what used to be the fire, cold and scattered now. The spider and tripod were gone, but the tent remained.

Mrs. Overton stood and almost smiled. "I am glad you made it. The tent is yours and whatever else you find. I have no need of anything to remind me of this place and what I lost here."

Whit wondered if that included Tad. He hoped not.

He stepped off Oro, dropped the reins and reached into his waistcoat. "This is for your livestock." He handed her the money and waited as she counted through it. With a tight jaw he disregarded the insult since she was a woman.

"And this is for the land." He unfolded the bill.

Tad reached for it. Whit snatched it away and drilled

the boy with a hard look. Tad melted back and his mother held out her hand. Whit gave her the money. "As agreed."

She nodded.

"Do you have papers?"

The woman withdrew a folded paper from her skirt pocket and handed it to Whit. Without another word, she and her son walked to the wagon, climbed up and drove away. They did not look back.

Suddenly alone, Whit exhaled what he recognized as relief. He had not asked the layout of the property, but the papers in his hand would say. He slipped them inside his waistcoat to read later.

The camp huddled in a small meadow a hundred yards from the full-running stream he had crossed. Grass-covered hills swelled around it like gently cupped hands, and behind them rose the timbered ridges and rock-strewn mountains common to the area.

A nice spot. A place that could be home if a man had the right woman. Livvy's scent brushed by and he turned, expecting to see her standing near him. But it was just the breeze playing tricks with his heart.

He walked around the cabin. No floor. He'd lay Livvy a wood floor, someday a fine carpet like her grandmother's. And build her a real house.

He hadn't even found the Overtons' cows yet and here he was dreaming away the daylight.

A muffled sound jerked his head toward the tent and his heart to a stop. He laid his right hand against his holster and eased toward the shabby shelter. Was there a coyote poking around?

There—again. His fingers curled around the butt of his pistol and he pulled it from the leather, cocked the hammer. With the barrel he pushed the tent flap aside. He squinted as his eyes adjusted to the dark interior. And then he saw it.

A black-and-white head poked out beneath a cot. Two

white paws inched forward and a whimper followed. A small dust cloud rose at the swish of a tail.

Whit eased back the hammer and slipped his gun in the holster. He squatted. The animal looked away, the paws scooted forward, and the whimper repeated.

Kind eyes. Not spooked or wild. Whit held out his left hand. "Come on, fella."

The whimper strengthened to a yearning that tugged at Whit's gut. How could they leave a dog behind?

"...and whatever else you find."

Whit edged forward, hand outstretched. He didn't need a dog, especially not one that cowered.

The animal bellied its way out, hope and distrust mingled in its black eyes.

Whit lowered his voice. "Come on, boy. It's all right. You're safe now."

At the sound of promise, the dog crawled to Whit's hand and tucked its head beneath his fingers. Whit rubbed the smooth head, the ears. The dog wiggled closer and soon Whit had both hands on it, running them over the bony back, feeling every rib and yearning to get his hands on Tad Overton.

His throat tightened and he swallowed an egg-size knot. "What's your name, fella?"

By now the dog stood to its full height, a youngster, not more than a yearling, maybe less. Its feathery tail wagged like a parade flag, and hungry eyes drank in Whit as if he were God himself.

"Lord, what am I gonna do with a dog?" He remembered the rolled hotcake in his saddlebag. "Guess that's an answer, isn't it."

Whit slowly rose and backed through the tent opening, then walked to Oro lipping at grass a few feet away. He pulled out his stash and turned to see the pup sitting behind him, head cocked, ears up. One ear flopped at the tip, sign of a not-grown dog.

"A sharp one, you are." Whit held out the rolled cake and the dog sniffed once before inhaling the offering in one swift bite.

"Don't choke on it." Whit laughed out loud. Baker had told him nearly the same thing an hour earlier. He stood, gathered Oro's reins and swung into the saddle.

"You comin' or stayin'?" Fool question for sure, but he'd soon learn if the dog was the fool or not. A small yip answered and the pup wagged its tail.

Whit rode toward an open draw that led to the gorge. After a ways he looked over his shoulder. The dog trotted behind, far enough back not to spook the horse or get kicked.

No fool there.

A wide park opened on the other side of Eight Mile Mountain, and Whit followed its western reach into the high country. After an hour it narrowed between rocky ridges and sidled up alongside the Arkansas as it churned down the mountain, white topped and roaring through rocky stretches, placid and smooth in others. Like a certain woman he knew.

Just as the valley opened out at Texas Creek, he turned Oro down toward the river, through the brush and juniper. A hunch told him where he thought men might build a rock fortress. He was right, but no one was there.

The stonework stood mute and unmanned. The new rail lay not far from the abutment, but without ceremony or defender. The dog trotted closer, sniffed around the rock work and looked at Whit as if to ask the purpose.

"You're right. Pointless. Absolutely good for nothing."

Whit reined his horse through the trees and headed upstream. Martin Thatcher's spread lay along Texas Creek.

He'd turn in there, see if they had any word on where the railroad crews were.

An hour later, Whit urged Oro into an easy lope toward Cañon City. The dog ran beside him on the rutted road, its tongue hanging out and a near grin pulling at its jowls.

"You're a real maverick, aren't you?"

Black ears lifted and the dog looked up as if agreeing.

"You like that name?"

A slobbery grin.

"I'm talking to a dog."

Whit slowed to a walk, pulled off his hat and ran his sleeve across his forehead. Would Baker allow a dog called Maverick on the place? He snorted. Maverick pricked his ears. They'd soon find out.

It was late afternoon before they made it to town.

This was not how he had planned to spend early June— dragging into Cañon City with a half-dead dog, looking for a foolhardy boy who'd joined a gang of roughs fighting somebody else's war.

Martin Thatcher had told him both railroad crews had beat it into town and on to Pueblo and the roundhouse there. What were they going to do? Fight over the train station? They'd just blow a bunch of holes in each other.

But according to Thatcher, the Denver and Rio Grande boys and the Pueblo County sheriff intended to *borrow* the cannon from the armory and blow Masterson back to Kansas.

Whit turned Oro down the lane beside his father's church and rode back to the parsonage barn, where he watered Oro and Maverick and scooped cool trough water over his own head. Tired from riding and keeping a tight rein on his swirling emotions, he left Oro at the hitching rail and told Maverick to stay.

The dog dropped and laid its head on its paws with a

heavy sigh. If Jody Perkins had as much sense, Whit might be at home courting Livvy. Or at least trying to.

He slapped his hat against his thigh and stopped at the back porch steps by the columbines. They looked corralled, bunched together. Not free and spreading at the meadow's edge in aspen shade. But he knew his ma's love for the purple flower. Just like Livvy's.

The back door opened and his mother stepped out.

"What are you doing here?" A knife in one hand and a carrot in the other. If one didn't get him, the other would.

"Nice to see you, too, Ma."

Her tense shoulders relaxed and she tipped her head to the side with a sigh. "I'm sorry, Whit. But Livvy told us you couldn't come with her because of your work."

He combed his wet hair back with one hand, watched his mother's eyes narrow at the gesture and then drop to his sidearm.

"She was right," he said.

"And how is that, since here you are?"

Women sure had a way of complicating a man's life.

He moved up the steps, planted a kiss on her cheek and stepped past her into the kitchen. "Do you have any coffee left? I could use a cup."

His mother swept in with her usual grace and in no time had a full mug before him on the table. She poured a cup for herself, took the chair opposite and added sugar. Rather than a polite, silent stirring, the spoon clinked against the cup, indicating her concern.

"One of our hands, a boy about fourteen, lit out after the Denver railroad crew. Since we finished branding, I figured I could ride over to the river and haul him back by the ear. But they're gone. Every last one, and a rancher told me they all headed to the roundhouse in Pueblo, itching for a fight."

His mother seamed her lips, laid her hand on the family Bible. "I have been praying about this war." She slid a glance his way. "Among other things."

Whit was undoubtedly one of the other things.

"Appreciate that." He took a swig of the brew and held in a grimace. The pot had cooked down to horseshoe-floating thickness.

"Before sunup we heard them ride through town. Some in wagons, the rest on horseback. Your father is over at the mercantile now, trying to learn what he can." She raised worried eyes. "Do you think Tad Overton rode with them?"

Whit snorted. "Not unless he lit out after I saw him this morning."

"So he is at home, with his mother?" A two-sided question if Whit ever heard one, and the weightier side concerned his sister, Marti.

He glanced toward the stairs. His mother read the look.

"She is at the library, or so she says."

"Reading about dusty professors digging up dustier bones."

"Don't change the subject." She held him with that coppery gaze that had peeled the veneer off many a tall tale. He might as well cough up the whole sorry story.

"Overtons don't have a home anymore. I bought it."

She froze in her chair, her coffee cup halfway to her mouth. The copper gaze turned to brass. "You *what?*"

"The widow wanted off the land. Too many bad memories. I bought her cattle and Baker staked me on the land. It butts up next to the Bar-HB and we'll run the cows together."

She set the cup in its saucer and drew her hands into her lap. "Did the Overtons leave the area?"

"I wish I could say they had. But Doc Mason evidently needs a nurse, and the widow is fit for the job, according to Tad." He held the mug to his mouth, considered another swallow. "She didn't do much for the boy the day he was shot, but I guess I shouldn't fault a mother's fear."

"No, you should not." She raised a hand to her throat, fingered the open top button of her dress. "So they will be living in town."

"If Doc takes her on."

She took her cup to the sink and it clattered against the saucer. "Will you be staying to supper?"

The quiver in her voice decided him. "Yes." He loved his parents, but an unfamiliar urgency was starting to gnaw at his gut. He drenched it with a final swallow. "If you'll have me."

She turned with a tight smile. "Of course we will have you. You are always welcome." She tipped her head. "As is Livvy."

He was wrong. It wasn't a smile she wore, standing there with her arms folded across her waist. It was the leer of a professional inquisitor.

Chapter 18

The ranch house, barn and outbuildings reached across the verdant meadow like welcoming arms. Livvy's heart swelled with longing. Not for home in her parents' fine Denver parsonage, but home here, on the ranch. With Whit.

She was ruined for city life. For buggy rides through the park, the stately brick church and girls her age paying more attention to their latest fashions than to her father's sermons.

Her father. The joyful bubble burst with a painful prick. The dear man had swept a rancher's daughter off to the city to be his bride and here he was losing his only child to that same rancher's foreman.

If he allowed it.

Panic tightened her chest and inched up her throat. Pop might have made his opinion known where Whit was concerned, but her father did not even know she and Whit had been working so closely. Of course he knew Whit worked for her grandfather, but he didn't *know*...

Oh, dear.

At least Tad Overton was already gone when she'd stopped at Doc Mason's. His ma had come for him, Doc said as he took Pop's money.

Livvy was relieved. She could drive faster without a wounded passenger to worry about. She slapped Bess into a jolting lope and every board in the wagon squawked in protest.

Pulling the mare up in a dust cloud at the barn, Livvy looped the reins on the brake and leaped, very unladylike, from the board. Skirts were such a nuisance. She grabbed the leather satchel and marched into the barn.

The shady interior hung like night and she blinked several times, willing her eyes to adjust to the dim alleyway. The stalls stood empty and no one worked on anvil or tack. She strode to the side that opened into the corrals and the near pasture, counted the horses.

One was missing. A tall black-stockinged buckskin.

She hurried to the house and stopped at the kitchen door with her pulse pounding in her ears. Gripping the satchel's handle, she pulled clean mountain air in through her nose and concentrated on slowing her heartbeat. With one hand she shook out her skirts and checked her braid to find it still coiled in place. Another deep breath and she reached for the doorknob.

Pop's voice boomed from his study, rolled around the dining room and shot into the kitchen. "That you, Livvy?"

She closed the door quietly behind her, determined not to match his uproarious greeting though she wanted nothing more than to run through the house like Marti would, jump into his lap and confess her affection for his foreman.

Glancing at the table, untidy sideboard and stove top, she continued into the dining room, noted the wilted lilacs on the dusty table, and stopped at the door to her grandfather's study. "Hello, Pop."

Poise. Grace. Restraint. She drew them all together like ribbons on a package and pinned on a smile. "Did you miss me?"

The man looked up and his gray eyes sparkled. "You are a bright flower among dull sagebrush. Come here, child."

Delighted by his tender greeting, she pulled the mail from her satchel, dropped the bag by the door and walked to his chair. He folded her into his still-powerful arms in a great bear hug.

"We missed you, Livvy."

We?

"I was gone for only a day and night. Surely you could get by without my cooking for that long."

"Not just your cooking." He held her at arm's length and gave her a squinted appraisal. "I do believe you are more beautiful than when you left. Just like your mother and Mama Ruth."

She giggled and worked free of his hands. "You are trying to get on my good side so I'll give you fresh biscuits and Annie Hutton's apple butter."

He leaned back against his leather chair and twisted one side of his mustache. "That was mighty good, what you left behind. We finished it off."

"So soon?" She laid the mail on his desk. "I should have known. And my guess is that Buck ate the most."

He grunted. "Not a chance with Whit keeping the jar at his plate, a knife in one hand and a sour eye on anyone daring to reach for it."

Laughter bubbled up and she walked back to the door. "I have your liniment here, and two more jars of apple butter. But I'll need Whit and Buck to unload the supplies."

Pop's mustache fell and jerked her hopes down with it. *Breathe.* "Where are they? Out chasing mavericks?"

"I imagine Buck has his boots off at the bunkhouse." Pop stood. "I'll go get him."

"Can't Whit do that?" *Why* couldn't Whit do that?

Her grandfather stopped directly in front of her and held her with a loving gaze. "He's gone after Jody."

A gasp slipped away before she could forbid it and her right hand tightened on the satchel handle.

"Now, don't you worry. That Whit's got a fine head on his shoulders, don't doubt that for a minute."

It wasn't his shoulders she was worried about. "Where did he go?" *Not the railroad war. Please, not the war.*

"Overtons told him Jody joined up with the Santa Fe boys layin' track."

If she did not sit she would faint and show her grandfather she was no better than the wilting lilacs. She leaned against the doorframe, afraid to attempt the great distance to the nearest chair.

Pop took her by the arm and led her to the dining table, where he pulled out a ladder-back chair. Grateful, she fell into it and clutched the satchel to her breast as if it held all her strength and fortitude rather than tooth powder, a hairbrush and Annie's apple butter.

Pop took the next chair and turned it to face her. "Whit left the same morning you did with a couple things on his mind." At that, the man's eyes snapped with a private notion and his silver mustache jerked to one side. "He has some news I am sure he wants to tell you himself rather than have me spill the beans."

Curiosity gained a foothold on worry and Livvy relaxed her death grip on the bag.

"No, I am not going into that—" he raised a callused hand "—so don't ask me. But you should know that he is determined to bring Jody back from the rail war."

Livvy tightened her arms around the satchel again and considered pulling out Pop's liniment to use as a smelling salt.

"He might be gone for a few days. But I'm sure he will

be safe." Pop fingered his mustache and nodded with a far-off look over her shoulder. "I've seen him use that Winchester a time or two."

Maybe her grandfather *wanted* her to swoon, fall out right there across Mama Ruth's beautiful dining room carpet.

Oh, Lord, please. Don't let Whit get involved in the railroad war. Please!

Whit's ma's chicken pot pie was bested only by his grandmother's, and Whit raised a hearty amen after grace as he set about proving it. It was a wonder his pa wasn't as big as a horse for his ma's great cooking and a preacher's sedate lifestyle. But the Reverend Caleb Hutton had never been one to simply sit by and let other men do the hard labor. Townsfolk still called on him when their foaling mares were having a hard time.

The man had a reputation. Whit chuckled around a mouthful at the oft-told family story about how his dad had delivered a foal during his first Christmas Eve service in Cañon. Dolly, his ma had named the filly, and they had her still.

Soon he and Livvy would be creating their own tales.

He hoped.

Suddenly sobered by the reminder that he needed to talk to Livvy's father, he cut a glance at his own. "You going to Denver any time soon?"

Marti, always two steps ahead of everybody else's thought processes, held him in a calculating gaze. "What's got you wanting to go to Denver?"

Whit straightened his back, hoping to bully her with his bigger bulk. She intimidated as easily as Livvy—not at all.

His pa took a hearty bite and closed his eyes as he chewed, clearly relishing his wife's handiwork before he replied. "Not any time soon. I want to stay close until this train war is cleared up."

Whit's ma made a clucking sound in her throat and Marti's attention suddenly fell to her half-empty plate.

"I understand that is the reason for your visit," his pa said.

Guilt poked Whit like a pitch fork. He could take time to follow a fool boy into town but not for a legitimate visit with his folks. He coughed hard and ran the napkin across his mouth.

"Yes, sir, it is." He glanced at his mother, who was pushing piecrust around on her plate. "Ma said you heard men ride through here early this morning, before daylight. Did you happen to look out and see anything? Specifically a stout little black horse with a white blaze?"

His pa nodded. "Didn't look out, but I saw that horse at this livery this afternoon. One of yours?"

That characteristic calm set Whit on edge—the way it always had. Rarely did his pa get excited about anything. A fine quality in a preacher, Whit supposed, but there were times when it drove him crazy with impatience.

He forced himself to stay seated, not dash out the door and run across the street to the livery. "More than likely." But what was it doing here if Jody rode with the railroad men?

A sudden pounding at the front door jerked Marti from her chair before their ma could tell her to keep her seat. Whit followed, grateful for an excuse to use his legs.

Marti had the door opened wide to a breathless boy standing on the threshold.

"Mr. Sutton told me to run this to the pastor." The boy gulped a quick breath. "He in?"

"I'll take it for him." Whit stopped next to his sister and held out his hand.

The boy's chest heaved beneath his galluses, but he gripped the telegram tightly.

Whit scowled.

His father came from the kitchen. "Thank you, William. Tell Mr. Sutton I appreciate it." He slipped a coin into the boy's hand and the youngster repaid him with a grin and dashed across the porch, down the path and into the lane toward Main Street.

No wonder he waited for Pa.

Whit closed the door and followed his sister to the kitchen, where they all resumed their seats. His pa laid the telegram beside his plate and picked up his coffee. A bronc-y gleam danced in his eyes as he ignored his baited family.

"Pa-ah!" Marti spoke for everyone, and for once Whit appreciated her impudence.

"Caleb, really." His ma chided her husband. "Tell us what it says."

"Oh, you mean this?" He lifted the thin folded paper.

Marti stamped her foot underneath the table.

"Martha Mae, hold your foot." Whit's ma fought her own battles against foot stomping and he grabbed his coffee cup to hide that bit of knowledge.

Slowly and deliberately, his pa unfolded the paper and silently read the message, moving his lips as he did so. Marti made growling noises and Whit's ma scraped her shoes back and forth on the braided rug beneath the table.

"'DRG to armory with Sheriff Price to commandeer cannon. Masterson and ATSF in possession. Stormed telegraph office. Shots fired. On to roundhouse. Masterson surrendered. Most well.'"

"Most well?" Whit's ma held trembling fingers to her lips. "Does that mean someone was shot?"

Pa refolded the paper and slipped it into his waistcoat. "Most likely we will know more tomorrow. But it sounds like it didn't turn into the bloodbath I feared, thank the Lord."

"But who stormed the telegraph office?" Marti's eyes flashed with a mix of excitement and fear.

"I heard talk at the mercantile that the Denver crew rode to Pueblo to seize the cannon. But this telegram says that Masterson and the Santa Fe men already had it."

"Then why did Masterson surrender?" Whit could make no more sense of the telegram than his sister and mother.

"We'll have to wait until our so-called posse returns to get the whole story. And I am certain that it will be the talk of the town for weeks. The trick will be getting the story straight once we start hearing those men boast and gloat."

Whit's mother went to the sideboard and returned with a vinegar pie.

His mouth watered for the "in-between" dessert they always ate before the peaches came in. She must be saving her strawberries for jam.

"But who won?" She sliced a hearty serving for each member of the family. "If you can call it winning."

Whit's pa laid a gentle hand on his wife's arm and looked into her worried eyes. "I'd say the town won."

As good an answer as any, at least until they had more details.

Whit cut into his pie and let the sweet custard and flaky crust melt in his mouth. The railroad would run through the mountain's heart to Leadville—one way or another. He'd prefer men not die over it. Especially young men.

If some hadn't already.

The next morning Whit left before sunup and stopped at the livery. The whoosh of Pete's billows seeped through the crack in the massive barn doors. The smithy was getting a head start before the day's heat vied with his furnace, and the twang of hot metal nipped Whit's nose as he tied Oro at the rail.

Whit walked the alleyway, checking each stall for a stout black gelding with a white blaze. He found it in the fourth stall, feeding on grass hay.

"Mornin', Whit." The ping of hammer on iron punctuated the man's greeting. "What brings you into town so early?"

Whit stopped near the anvil, watched Pete's massive arm flex as he gripped an L-shaped piece and shoved it into the fire.

"Stayed at my folks' last night and I wanted to see you about a job before I left today."

The blacksmith withdrew the glowing iron from the coals, laid it over the anvil's horn and hammered it around. "What kind of job?"

"I need a brand."

Pete glanced up, repositioned the piece. "The Bar-HB got so many cows they need another iron?"

Whit pushed his hat back, already warm so close to the fire. "It's for me. I'm starting my own herd."

The blacksmith set his hammer down, laid the piece across the anvil and mopped his sweaty face with a rag. "Show me."

Whit squatted and smoothed the finely ground dust with his hand. Then he drew the double H with a wide inverted V across the top.

"Like a rafter," Pete said, looking over Whit's shoulder.

"Wider. It's a mountain. Spreads over both letters here." Whit retraced the angled bars indicative of a mountain peak.

Whit stood, wiped his hand on his pants. "Any way I can get it today?"

Pete folded his arms across his thick chest. "This afternoon."

Whit was hoping to be home near noon. "No sooner?"

A thick arm swept toward the anvil. "I have shoes to make. This afternoon is the best I can do."

"This afternoon it is. I'll be back."

He repositioned his hat, and remembering his other task, jerked his chin toward the alleyway. "Who brought in the black gelding?"

Pete picked up his hammer and chuckled. "I saw the Bar-HB when the sheriff brought it in. Wondered how it got all the way down the mountain with a saddle and no rider."

Whit's throat tightened. "Sheriff? No rider?" What was funny about that?

"Then he told me he locked the boy in the jailhouse. Said to keep the horse until the Denver railroad crew got back from Pueblo. Even paid me."

"He being the sheriff?"

Pete nodded, grabbed the tongs and shoved the curved iron back into the fire. "You going to take the black with you?"

Whit dragged his hand over his face. "Yeah, I'll take him when I leave. Put that brand on Baker's tab. I'll square up with him."

Pete returned to his work. Whit headed for the door and fresh air.

Dawn flushed the horizon and he thought of the cougar. Hoped she hadn't taken another calf while he was gone. Hoped even more that Baker hadn't heard her scream and gone out looking for her. The urgency returned, chewing at his gut. He had to get back.

He swung into the saddle and turned Oro toward the mercantile. His grandfather would already be there with the coffee hot.

Chapter 19

A cow bellowed and Livvy's eyelids fluttered open. Sparrows chittered from the lilac bush near her window, and she burrowed beneath her quilt, listening, delighted to be back on the ranch. In the next breath, worry nibbled a hole in her comfort. Was Whit back? Or was he still riding the countryside looking for Jody Perkins and meeting up with God knew who?

Oh, Lord, please, please protect him.

Throwing off the quilt, she sat up and stretched her arms above her head. Her Bible lay open on the small table, and a ribbon marked the passage she had read the night before. She reached for it and looked again at the words Whit's mother had shared.

"'Trust in the Lord with all thine heart; and lean not unto thine own understanding.'"

Trusting God with her eternal soul had been easy for Livvy. She had been raised to take Him at His word, and she believed what He said about salvation. It all made sense to her—God's gift of love and forgiveness in Jesus. But trusting Him with her *heart* where Whit was concerned? For some reason that was harder.

"Oh, Lord, please protect Whit from gunmen and from his own brash ways." Tears pricked her eyes and she knuckled them away. What choice did she have other than to trust God? She looked again at the passage. *Lean not on thine own understanding.*

That was her only option, and she knew full well that her own understanding fell far short on so many things. She could not see Whit at the moment. She could not perceive his thoughts, nor did she know his next move. She didn't even know where he was.

"Forgive me, Lord. Help me trust You even with this."

Fear pressed in and took a bite. If she truly placed Whit in the Lord's hand and removed her own clutching fingers, she could lose him. What if God chose not to bring him home safely? What if a future with Whit was not in God's plan for her life? What then?

She closed the Bible and laid it on the table, determined to commit the verse to memory as Annie Hutton had. Maybe that would calm her quaking heart.

She washed and dressed for the day and tied her hair back with a blue ribbon. In the kitchen she grabbed the egg basket and headed for the henhouse.

Sweet mountain air filled her lungs and dew sparkled on the fence posts and lilac bushes—even on the weeds that had taken up residence in the garden during a week's neglect. She'd pay dearly for three days' branding and two days in town. But Buck's prickly new fence looked to be holding out the deer.

She lined the basket with pink rhubarb stalks then went to the coop, where she found the red hen napping atop her clutch. Livvy cooed to the old bird as she slipped a hand beneath her feathery roundness and counted six warm eggs.

"He shall cover thee with his feathers, and under his wings shalt thou trust."

The old childhood verse flew across the years. Again, trust. "Oh, Lord," she whispered to the setting hen, "help me trust You."

Livvy blinked away the persistent tears and stepped back, watching the docile creature on her nest. She knew what a vicious defender the wise old mother could be.

How much more so the Lord?

Forcing herself from thought into action, Livvy quickly cleaned out the remaining nests and left the coop. Daylight was burnin', as Whit would say. Her heart tugged at the thought of his warm voice.

And Buck Perkins tugged at the back door, stomping his feet on the step. Livvy cleared her throat loud enough to be heard. He jerked a look over his shoulder and opened the door wide, stepping aside for her to enter.

"Thank you, Buck. And thank you for washing before you come inside."

His mumbled "yes, ma'am" faded behind the closing door and she smiled at his reticence. She'd make a civilized man out of that boy if it was the last thing she did.

The morning flew by with rhubarb and egg-custard pies, cinnamon cookies, and the scrubbing of what had not been scrubbed in a week. By then it was time to feed Pop and Buck again. As soon as she finished cleaning up after dinner, she hung her apron over a chair back, went to her room and traded her blue calico dress for a blouse and Mama Ruth's denims. She'd forgo the hat with the sun edging away toward the western peaks.

Pop snoozed in his desk chair, his stocking feet crossed on the desk blotter and his mustache ruffling as he snored. She smiled as she eased past the door, deciding not to wake him. She'd be back in an hour or two, in plenty of time to serve leftovers, bread and apple butter. And more pie.

Maybe it was habit that prompted her to saddle Ranger rather than another horse. He had proved such a stalwart fellow during the branding. His surefootedness comforted her, and he wisely avoided badger holes long before she even saw them. She could ride Ranger and relax, enjoy the mountain beauty without being overly alert. And that was exactly what she wanted to do.

Livvy set the sturdy gray to a leisurely walk and angled him across the wide meadow toward the rimrock. Cottonwoods clustered along the base of the red wall and she expected to find columbines hiding in their shade.

As she approached with the sun at her back, the blue curtain above the rimrock hung in sharp contrast to the red cliffs and quivering green trees. Wilson Creek chattered contentedly nearby.

Ranger's ears pricked forward and he raised his head toward the nearing wall. Livvy tried to follow his gaze, but saw only the multihued strata of rock and sediment laid down over the centuries. Perhaps a deer or mountain sheep had disturbed a rock and sent it tumbling to catch the horse's keen hearing.

In a moment, he relaxed his neck and plodded onward, matching Livvy's peaceful demeanor. She marveled at such color so far from town, more varied and brilliant than any dressmaker's work or gaily painted house. And with the afternoon sun shining directly on the scene, the rocks and trees and grass shimmered with near incandescence.

Tranquility embraced her. No shouting freight drivers rattling their wagons. No rowdy miners. No bickering women haggling over a merchant's prices. No people sounds at all. Simply peace.

A sigh escaped her lips and she settled even deeper into the saddle.

The trees were farther than she anticipated—a phenomenon she had noticed during the branding. The clear air made the mountains and ridges appear closer than they really were. But as she approached her expectations were rewarded, and she spotted fragile purple heads clustered in gossipy groups.

She stopped at the clearing's edge, and Ranger immediately began lipping the tender grass. She untied the old flour bag she had brought for holding columbines on the return trip. A heavy cooking spoon, perfect for digging, weighted it down.

She slipped to the ground and dropped Ranger's reins, ground tying the well-trained horse as Whit had demonstrated.

Intent on her hunt, she stepped carefully through the patch, stopping at the most prolific clusters. The afternoon waned without her notice, but a distant cloud's pass across the sun alerted her to the fading day. One more plant, then home.

An unexpected pile of leaves and brush caught her eye, and she turned aside to inspect it. A persistent buzzing hung above the leaves and a septic odor wafted her way. Odd that she would smell an open wound here in the meadow so far from people.

Whit's words at breakfast two weeks ago hit her memory like a rifle shot. *"I found her latest kill in the cottonwoods, half covered with leaves and brush."*

The breath froze in her lungs and she stopped dead still. The hair on her arms rose and a spidery shiver crawled up her back. Someone—or something—was watching her.

Whit made Jody Perkins ride next to him on the way to the ranch. Maverick trotted drag, unaware of the insulting position and grinning as if happy to be included at all.

Jody sat his horse like a seed-corn sack, slump shouldered and sullen. Three times before they cleared town Whit convinced himself not to whip the stuffing out of the boy. Buck and Baker would more than likely see to that.

Jody had to keep reining in the black. It was determined to lead. During those times he checked the horse with quick jerks on the reins, Whit studied the pride-busted boy. Was he mad at being found in the calaboose or was he mad that the Denver crew and Sheriff Price hadn't let him ride with them to Pueblo? Price had convinced the local magistrate to lock up the boy to keep him from following.

Whit snorted. Jody Perkins didn't know how lucky he was.

A heavy sun hung in the late-afternoon sky by the time they made the ranch road. The boy hadn't said two words and that suited Whit just fine. He had other things on his mind.

If he didn't care so much for his horse and the black, he'd over-and-under it all the way home. His scalp itched and it wasn't due to his pa's trough water. It was deeper. His blood simmered with warning. Danger stalked, yet when he checked their surroundings he found nothing suspicious. And Oro gave no sign that predators lurked. Even Maverick was unaffected, though his carefree countenance could simply mean he had as much sense as Jody Perkins and wouldn't know a mad bear if one slapped him on the rump.

Whit reached for his Winchester, slid it partway from the scabbard, slid it back in. He did the same with the Colt on his hip, made sure the pull was smooth and unhindered. He flexed his right hand and the gesture drew a worried glance from Jody.

Served him right.

Whit's nerves bunched in his legs and his back and he urged Oro into an easy lope. Another half hour and they should see the barn roof and the rimrock across the valley.

Rimrock. The word rippled through his arms and down his back. He was more nervous than a prairie dog at a badger picnic.

Watch her, Lord. Please, watch out for Livvy until I get there. Keep her safe.

Until he got there? What an arrogant prayer—as if he had more say-so than the Almighty. Maybe there was a bite of truth in Livvy's stinging reprimands. He needed to trust the Lord more and stop thinking everything depended on his doings. But that'd be a whole lot easier if he could see Livvy from where he sat atop his good horse.

When they loped into the yard, the place was deserted. No Buck, no Baker, no Livvy. No lights in the house and the sun had pulled itself behind the first peaks. Before long it would tuck tail and run for cover of night.

"Check the house for Buck and Livvy," he told Jody. "I'll check the corral and pasture."

The boy hit the ground running, apparently charged by the urgency in Whit's voice.

Whit loped to the barn and around to the back pasture. Baker's gray was gone. Either Whit's boss or his bride-to-be was out riding.

Jody ran out the kitchen door and halfway to the barn before he yelled, "Neither one's here. Just the boss."

Buck's horse was in the barn. That left Livvy out alone. Hurt? Trapped? Lost?

The yelling drew Buck from the bunkhouse, barefoot and shirtless. Whit slid Oro to a stop before him and tossed him the Colt. "Fire this three times if Livvy rides in." Buck held the gun as if it were hot iron and nodded so fast Whit thought his head would fly off.

He whirled Oro around and dug in his spurs. The buckskin lunged forward and landed on the gallop, straight for the shadowy red rimrock.

Baker's gray caught the last of daylight as Whit neared

the meadow's edge. He pulled to a trot, saw the horse's reins dragging as it grazed. At Whit's approach it jerked its head up and rumbled a greeting.

Livvy was nowhere.

Had she fallen? Had Ranger thrown her into some spot Whit couldn't see in the fading light? Or was she off climbing the outcroppings, getting herself in a fix?

And then he saw her yellow hair. She stood a hundred feet beyond the gray, against a bank of cottonwood trees, as still as stone, looking down. Every fiber in Whit's body wanted to run to her and sweep her into his arms, but his instincts told him to look closer.

Only the cottonwood leaves moved, fluttering in the early-evening breeze. And a long golden rope that whipped soundlessly from side to side atop a small pile of boulders.

Whit's blood froze in his veins. A shout formed in his throat but he checked it.

He drew out the rifle, cocked the hammer and took aim. The gray's ear swiveled at the metallic click. Livvy didn't move.

Daylight faded by degrees. He hadn't warned Livvy about riding out alone at dusk. How could he have been so careless? Why hadn't he hunted that cat down when he had the chance?

Regret dug its rowels deep. *Oh, Lord, please protect her.*

His finger hugged the trigger as he sighted left of the boulder that hid the cat's body. Only the movement of its tail betrayed its position. If he shot too soon he'd miss. If he shot too late—

Slowly, calmly, Livvy raised her head and looked at him. She knew.

Don't run, Livvy, darlin'. Don't run. How he loved her! Helplessness burned a hole through his heart as she turned. Her gasp reached his ears as her hands reached her face.

The cat leaped. Whit fired.

The rifle's report bounced off the rimrock and set Ranger to prancing. Whit kicked Oro into a run and jerked up next to Livvy on the ground beneath the lion.

He jumped down, never taking his aim off the cat. Stretched Livvy's length, its tongue lolled across her hair. Blood soaked her blouse.

Neither of them moved.

He kicked at a plate-size back paw. No response.

"Livvy." The word scraped up his throat, dragging his soul with it.

Keeping his finger on the trigger, he stooped beside her, laid a hand on the lion to feel for its breath. Satisfied the animal was dead, he knelt and rolled the cat off Livvy and his heart stopped.

Her chest barely rose with each shallow breath. Red cuts swelled on the back of her hands where claws had slashed, and the stripes widened and spilled into rivulets that ran down her arms.

He choked out her name and lifted her to him. Once against his chest, she melted in his embrace and began to sob from behind her hands.

"You came. I thought—I thought—"

"It's all right now, darlin'. You're safe. I've got you." He kissed the top of her head, felt her heart pounding against his. *Oh, God, you guarded her steps and prodded me on. Thank You. With all my life, I thank You.*

Gently, he lifted the fingers of one hand, afraid of what he'd find. But her fair face bore only the wash of her tears.

"We need to get you back to the house. Take care of these scratches on your hands."

A great soundless sob racked her body and she lowered the other hand. "What scratches?"

More like gouges. They dripped onto the denims she was so proud of, and when Livvy saw them she cried out.

Whit pulled off his neckerchief and wrapped it around her right hand, the more deeply cut of the two. Then he stood, easily lifting her in his arms. "Can you ride?"

She nodded. Of course she'd say yes. He was proud of her stubbornness but he couldn't have her passing out. "I'm going to put you on Oro. I'll sit behind you and lead Ranger back." He looked deep into her shining eyes, so round and terror filled. "Are you sure you can sit the saddle?"

She nodded slowly, determined. "Yes," she whispered. "I can do it."

Chapter 20

Livvy hadn't been waited on since she was twelve and sick with a fever. But she had no say in the matter. The laudanum Pop administered at annoyingly regular intervals left her head fuzzy.

Whit was worse, seeing to the bandages that swathed both hands, tenderly changing them each morning, and even more tenderly applying a healing salve.

But more healing than Doc Mason's cure-all ointment was the love in Whit's eyes. If he never spoke the words in her lifetime, she knew he loved her. The admission spilled over with every touch and every smoky glance that sent shivers coursing through her.

She yearned for him.

And he knew it.

For that she could kick him, and would if she could stand without feeling light-headed and woozy. Yet for all her fussing and grousing, she thanked God for Whit's attention and Pop's medication.

Only twice since the attack had she wakened in the night with a cold, incalculable fear clutching her heart. She must have cried out, for both times her grandfather had come immediately, murmuring soothing words, assuring her she was safe, tucking the quilt around her as if she were a child again.

But in the daylight she had been remarkably calm. "Resting" once again with her legs extended on the dining room settee, she adjusted her skirt, flexing her fingers to force the stiffness from them.

Her hands would always be scarred. When she'd held them unbandaged before the mirror, side by side as they had been that day against her face, the red swath of three razorlike claws declared how close she'd come to disfigurement. To death. The cuts were smooth, deep, precise.

She'd never understand why she had raised her hands. But she didn't have to understand. God's timing had been even more precise than the lion's attack.

Restless rather than restful, she swung her legs down and stretched her back, considering a trek to the kitchen to check on the pantry.

Every morning for a week Buck had faithfully delivered a basketful of warm eggs. But the morning he discovered hatchlings peeking beneath the old red hen, he strutted more than the rooster.

"You should see them babies," he cackled at breakfast.

"*Those* babies," Livvy murmured.

Buck shot her a shy glance. "Yes, ma'am. Those babies."

"You act like you had something to do with 'em." Pop's mustache twitched and his eyes twinkled.

Buck blushed and ducked his head. "I did. I left her alone."

Whit snorted. "After she nearly peeled the skin off your hand the first time you reached in there."

Jody hooted, fitting in more comfortably than he had

for a few days. Pop and Buck had worn him out, and he'd no doubt think twice before he lit out after any more hired guns.

Livvy awkwardly spread apple butter across one of Pop's famous hotcakes, getting more on the plate than the cake. Whit reached to help her and she stopped him with a deadly glare. He smirked and withdrew his hand before it suffered the same fate as hers, but from a well-aimed fork.

She chuckled at the memory, ready to stand when Pop came out of his study and straight at her with a bottle and spoon. She shooed him off.

"I am done with that, thank you very much. I must get my mind clear, and you've got me all cloudy and befuddled with that whiskey you're giving me."

He stopped short, stared at the bottle, then held the label side toward her. "It is *not* whiskey. See here? It's laudanum."

"Oh, Pop, I'm teasing you. But I cannot take any more. I need to start thinking straight. Why, I could barely make sense of the newspaper article about the train war."

He grunted and stuffed the cork back in the bottle. "Makes no difference, if you ask me. Far as I can tell, Masterson went back to Kansas. Some folks think he was paid off. But I think he got smart and figured he'd let the train barons fight it out." He raised a bushy brow. "Denver did have a court order, you know. Proved they had the right-of-way through the gorge."

No, she did not know, but it sounded about right that a bunch of roughs on both sides had worked themselves up for a fight that was already won.

"Won't be long until we hear the whistle all the way up here when the train runs through to Leadville." He lumbered back to his study and returned with an envelope.

"This was in the mail you brought. Didn't you see it?"

Livvy took the envelope and read the return address.

"Mother and Daddy. No, I didn't." She looked at her dear grandfather. "Thank you. I must have been too distracted over the rail-war news to notice."

She held out the envelope. "Open it for me, please?"

With a jerk of his mustache and a quick swipe of his stock knife, Pop handed back the letter. "I'll be in the study if you need me."

Livvy unfolded the thin paper, smelled her mother's light rosy scent, and read news of her parents and home. Their lives were the same—the daily duties of a pastor and his wife. She missed them, but she did not miss Denver. A frown drew her brows as she read of their plans to visit in the fall. Did they expect her to return home with them?

The kitchen door opened and a familiar boot step crossed the floor and stopped at the dining room. Livvy looked up at the handsome cowboy, hat cocked to the side, a confident gleam in his eye.

Her pulse quickened. "Have you come to take me beyond the bounds of these crushing walls, Mr. Hutton?"

A slow smile spread. "'Bout time you got off your pretty pastime, don't you think, Miss Hartman?"

She fanned the letter in front of her face, inflamed by his forward remark. "Really. Such language."

Whit strode across the floral carpet to the settee and bent to scoop her up.

She resisted. "My legs work just fine."

Bent so close to her, he lifted one brow in an unspoken comment. Livvy flushed, certain she matched the burgundy cushion beneath her. She laid the letter aside and slipped a bandaged hand in the crook of Whit's arm as he straightened. "A walk would be lovely."

They exited the front door and strolled toward the barn. The fresh air invigorated her, reminded her that life existed beyond the confines of the ranch house. Reminded her of the beautiful, living country surrounding it.

Whit led her to a rough bench against the barn, shaded now in the afternoon light. He sat beside her, linked his left arm with her right one and cradled her bandaged hand in both of his. Then he raised her hand to his lips and kissed the palm side of her fingers.

A storm stirred in his eyes, as fierce and powerful as the squall that had pinned them at the rocks. His pulse pounded against her wrist and probed a vein in his neck, hammering a heavy counterpoint to her own running heartbeat.

"I love you, Olivia Hartman."

The husky voice rippled through her. "Well, I'd say it's about time you figured that out."

His eyes darkened, narrowed as he searched her face.

She touched his rough chin. "I love you, too, Whitaker Hutton. Whiskers and all."

He swallowed. "Would you marry a cowboy?"

Unable to resist the temptation, she rounded her eyes with innocence. "Do you have one in mind?"

He growled deep in his chest and slitted his eyes. She shivered in delight and laid her hand on his arm, holding his dangerous gaze.

"Will you marry *me?*"

She closed her eyes, relishing his words, words she had wondered if she'd ever hear. "With pleasure, Mr. Hutton."

She leaned toward him, expecting a kiss that never came, then scolded herself for being so brash and bold.

He released her hand, left her briefly, and returned with a canvas roll. Standing before her, he withdrew a long wooden-handled stamp iron she didn't recognize. Then he smoothed the dirt with his boot and stamped the brand. When he stepped back, a wide inverted V hung above twin *H*s.

Puzzled, she looked up.

"That's you and me—Hutton and Hartman—beneath the mountain. That's our brand."

"Our brand?" She leaned over to trace the imprinted dirt with her finger, a spark of joy flaring in her breast. "But we—you—have no cattle. Why do we need a brand?"

Gently he raised her and with his hands grasping her arms, leaned down and brushed his lips against hers. He pulled back and his breath warmed her face. "I bought out the widow Overton and your grandfather staked us on the land. We have our own herd now, our own place."

Peering into those stormy depths, she could feel the hail beating against her reason. "You—you had this made before you even asked me?" She stiffened at the realization. "You arrogant—"

Lightning struck and he pulled her against him, pressing his mouth to hers with a hunger that both startled and thrilled her. When he broke away, he buried his face in her hair with a hoarse whisper. "You had to say yes. What would I do with all those cows without you?"

Laughing, she wrapped her swathed hands around his neck and leaned back. "Confident, aren't you, Mr. Hutton." She kissed him heatedly, then drank in the love pouring from his eyes. "I'm sure you'll be needing my help come branding time."

He lifted her off the ground and swung her around with a cowboy's whoop that shot straight to her heart.

And that was exactly where she intended to keep him. Forever.

* * * * *

REQUEST YOUR FREE BOOKS!

2 FREE INSPIRATIONAL NOVELS
PLUS 2
FREE
MYSTERY GIFTS

Love Inspired®

YES! Please send me 2 FREE Love Inspired® novels and my 2 FREE mystery gifts (gifts are worth about $10). After receiving them, if I don't wish to receive any more books, I can return the shipping statement marked "cancel." If I don't cancel, I will receive 6 brand-new novels every month and be billed just $4.74 per book in the U.S. or $5.24 per book in Canada. That's a savings of at least 21% off the cover price. It's quite a bargain! Shipping and handling is just 50¢ per book in the U.S. and 75¢ per book in Canada.* I understand that accepting the 2 free books and gifts places me under no obligation to buy anything. I can always return a shipment and cancel at any time. Even if I never buy another book, the two free books and gifts are mine to keep forever.

105/305 IDN F49N

Name	(PLEASE PRINT)

Address	Apt. #

City	State/Prov.	Zip/Postal Code

Signature (if under 18, a parent or guardian must sign)

Mail to the Harlequin® Reader Service:
IN U.S.A.: P.O. Box 1867, Buffalo, NY 14240-1867
IN CANADA: P.O. Box 609, Fort Erie, Ontario L2A 5X3

**Are you a subscriber to Love Inspired books
and want to receive the larger-print edition?
Call 1-800-873-8635 or visit www.ReaderService.com.**

* Terms and prices subject to change without notice. Prices do not include applicable taxes. Sales tax applicable in N.Y. Canadian residents will be charged applicable taxes. Offer not valid in Quebec. This offer is limited to one order per household. Not valid for current subscribers to Love Inspired books. All orders subject to credit approval. Credit or debit balances in a customer's account(s) may be offset by any other outstanding balance owed by or to the customer. Please allow 4 to 6 weeks for delivery. Offer available while quantities last.

Your Privacy—The Harlequin® Reader Service is committed to protecting your privacy. Our Privacy Policy is available online at www.ReaderService.com or upon request from the Harlequin Reader Service.
We make a portion of our mailing list available to reputable third parties that offer products we believe may interest you. If you prefer that we not exchange your name with third parties, or if you wish to clarify or modify your communication preferences, please visit us at www.ReaderService.com/consumerschoice or write to us at Harlequin Reader Service Preference Service, P.O. Box 9062, Buffalo, NY 14269. Include your complete name and address.

LIDIR13R

REQUEST YOUR FREE BOOKS!

2 FREE INSPIRATIONAL NOVELS
PLUS 2
FREE
MYSTERY GIFTS

Love Inspired.
HISTORICAL
INSPIRATIONAL HISTORICAL ROMANCE

YES! Please send me 2 FREE Love Inspired® Historical novels and my 2 FREE mystery gifts (gifts are worth about $10). After receiving them, if I don't wish to receive any more books, I can return the shipping statement marked "cancel." If I don't cancel, I will receive 4 brand-new novels every month and be billed just $4.74 per book in the U.S. or $5.24 per book in Canada. That's a savings of at least 21% off the cover price. It's quite a bargain! Shipping and handling is just 50¢ per book in the U.S. and 75¢ per book in Canada.* I understand that accepting the 2 free books and gifts places me under no obligation to buy anything. I can always return a shipment and cancel at any time. Even if I never buy another book, the two free books and gifts are mine to keep forever.

102/302 IDN F5CY

Name	(PLEASE PRINT)	
Address		Apt. #
City	State/Prov.	Zip/Postal Code

Signature (if under 18, a parent or guardian must sign)

Mail to the **Harlequin® Reader Service:**
IN U.S.A.: P.O. Box 1867, Buffalo, NY 14240-1867
IN CANADA: P.O. Box 609, Fort Erie, Ontario L2A 5X3

Want to try two free books from another series?
Call 1-800-873-8635 or visit www.ReaderService.com.

* Terms and prices subject to change without notice. Prices do not include applicable taxes. Sales tax applicable in N.Y. Canadian residents will be charged applicable taxes. Offer not valid in Quebec. This offer is limited to one order per household. Not valid for current subscribers to Love Inspired Historical books. All orders subject to credit approval. Credit or debit balances in a customer's account(s) may be offset by any other outstanding balance owed by or to the customer. Please allow 4 to 6 weeks for delivery. Offer available while quantities last.

Your Privacy—The Harlequin® Reader Service is committed to protecting your privacy. Our Privacy Policy is available online at www.ReaderService.com or upon request from the Harlequin Reader Service.

We make a portion of our mailing list available to reputable third parties that offer products we believe may interest you. If you prefer that we not exchange your name with third parties, or if you wish to clarify or modify your communication preferences, please visit us at www.ReaderService.com/consumerschoice or write to us at Harlequin Reader Service Preference Service, P.O. Box 9062, Buffalo, NY 14269. Include your complete name and address.

LIHDIR13R

ReaderService.com

Manage your account online!

- Review your order history
- Manage your payments
- Update your address

> ### We've designed the Harlequin® Reader Service website just for you.

Enjoy all the features!

- Reader excerpts from any series
- Respond to mailings and special monthly offers
- Discover new series available to you
- Browse the Bonus Bucks catalog
- Share your feedback

Visit us at:

ReaderService.com